MW01520830

This book is a work of fiction. Names, characters, places and incidents are the product of the author's imagination or are used fictitiously. Any resemblance to actual events, locales or persons is entirely coincidental.

ISBN 978-1-7386940-0-6

ALL WE HAVE IS

Today

RHIANE HESLOP

PROLOGUE

Summer

2022

AUGUST 2022

Anna

Life is happening to everyone but me I think as I stand behind one of my closest friends, Sarah. She's draped in white lace while her fiancé slips a wedding ring on her finger and promises to always love her. I, on the other hand, am a hot mess in mint green chiffon.

The August heat is oppressive, and my curtain bangs are sticking to my forehead in a pool of sweat. Blood-thirsty mosquitoes are circling me as I surreptitiously smack them with my bouquet while also smiling for the photographer (who is basically doing parkour to get the kind of shot Sarah wants). What I want to know is how Sarah met the love of her life and got to the alter all in one year when my boyfriend and I haven't even gotten *close* to an alter in four years. I'm the third in line of eight bridesmaids and I'm the only one unmarried; even Sarah's youngest sister is married and she's only twenty-two!

At thirty-one, that feels like an unnecessary slap in the face.

I'm honestly starting to feel like marriage is an elite social club that I'm never going to be allowed into. It's like there's some secret to get in but no one will tell me what it is. Not even Google. There's over twenty million search results for *how to get your boyfriend to propose* but no real answers.

My eyes, still watering from the fake eyelash glue that got in them (note to self, never do my own eyelashes), survey the crowd of guests looking for Darren. There's over a hundred friends and family sitting in white folding chairs on the lawn of a winery and I know most of them, having been friends with Sarah since high school.

My eyes eventually find Darren's and when he catches me looking, he smiles. This is the man I want to marry, the man I've loved every day for the past four years. He makes me incredibly happy and yet when I smile back at him, it feels fake. Why doesn't *he* want to marry *me*? In all the time that Darren and I have been together, he hasn't even hinted at marriage. I kind of hoped he might propose last year on my thirtieth birthday but I got a spa day instead. Lovely but not a diamond. Since then, I've started comparing myself to other women – women who have a ring on their finger – and I try to figure out what they have that I don't. And when I see women with babies, well, that's even worse.

I know I'm only thirty-one (thirty-two in October actually but I'm trying not to think about that), but it already feels like time is running out. *Fast*. I really, *really* want to have a baby. Most of my friends are already *done* having kids. And I can't even get started. I want to marry Darren but that doesn't have to happen first. I'd take a baby over a ring right now. Not that I'd say *no* to a ring, just, you know, I'm DTF.

Sarah and her husband kiss with open mouths and too much tongue as the officiant introduces them as husband and wife. My best friend, Nat, who stands behind me, nudges me in the ribs; I can practically feel her rolling her eyes and I have to bite my lip to keep myself from laughing. I can always count on her to distract me when I need it the most. She knows how hard weddings and bridal showers – not to mention baby showers – have become for me. I reach a hand behind me, and she grasps it, giving it a quick squeeze and then we dutifully follow the bride and groom down the aisle as the guests cheer.

I can't quite meet Darren's eyes as I walk past him. I *love* our relationship – there's no reason *not* to get married. Actually, I think our relationship is stronger than most of our friend's marriages. So what is he waiting for? If Darren hasn't realized that I'm "the one" yet, will he ever? And how long am I going to wait for him to figure it out?

PART ONE

Winter

2023

1

JANUARY 2023

Anna

Oh my god. OH MY GOD! Is this what I think it is? I'm staring down at a black velvet box that I just found in Darren's dresser drawer beneath lonely socks and expired condoms. I lift the lid slowly and gasp at the solitaire diamond winking up at me. Holy crap. HOLY CRAP! After 5 years together, Darren is FINALLY going to propose!

Carefully, I put the box back where I found it and immediately call Nat. She answers on the third ring and before she can even say *hello* I am shouting excitedly at her, "get your butt over here! I have something I want to show you!"

"What? But I'm watching Outlander. Can't you just tell me over the phone?"

"Nope, no way. You're going to have to come over."

"What could be *so* important that you need to pull me away from sexy Jamie?"

"Natalie."

"Ok, ok, jeez, you don't have to use your mom voice on me," she half laughs, half grumbles.

Laughing, I tell her not to worry about putting a bra back on because Darren isn't home.

"Wouldn't matter if he was," she says, and I roll my eyes because that is SO not true. She only just stopped wearing a bra around *me* and we've been friends for almost two decades. I remember in high school she used to sleep in her bra hoping that it would somehow make her boobs bigger. It didn't work. She'll never be more than a B and she'll always secretly hate me for my C's. Even when Nat was pregnant with her son, she didn't get the cleavage she hoped for. Now she despises wearing bras; I think it's her way of protesting unfair genetics.

Ten minutes later Nat is at my door in pink pajama pants with white polka dots and a sweater so thick you'd never know she had boobs in the first place. Her short brown pixie cut is disheveled and she's taken her contacts out, instead sporting her wire-framed glasses that highlight her large toffee-coloured eyes.

"So, why did I give up my evening of Scottish soft-core porn?" She pushes past me into the house.

"Follow me," I head upstairs to my bedroom as Nat stomps up the stairs behind me. I find myself wishing I had hidden the piles of dirty laundry that litter the floor but oh well. I head to Darren's dresser and open the top drawer, once again taking out the velvet ring box.

"Oh shit, is that what I think it is?!" Nat's voice is several octaves higher than usual, and her face wears a look of shock. Come on, we all knew this was going to happen eventually, right? My eyes prick with tears and I try to will them not to fall.

"Anna, don't *cry*! This is it! It's finally happening!"

"I know," I sniffle. "And I'm so excited," but I choke with a sob on the last word. Nat pulls me into a side hug. "I'm fine, really, it's just been a long time waiting, you know?"

"I know. He took his sweet-ass-time but here you are! So are you going to open the box and let me see the ring already?"

"Yes, of course!"

When I open the box she holds a hand up to her eyes and jokes, "woah! I'm blinded by the light." I laugh. She leans over to take a closer look. "Damn girl, look at that thing sparkle."

"It's perfect."

"So where did you find it?"

"In his sock drawer. Of all places," I roll my eyes at his stupidity and I place the box back into the drawer. We head back downstairs and into the kitchen. Nat takes a seat at the island while I stand on the other side and pour us two glasses of wine. Suddenly she gasps and grasps my forearm, taking me by surprise and causing me to spill some of the rosé.

"Hawaii – he's going to do it in Hawaii! My god, so *romantic*."

"Oh my god, you're probably right! I *knew* this was going to be the best trip of my life." It's less than two months before Darren and I fly to Hawaii for a ten day vacation.

"I'm so excited for you! Now, I need you to get pregnant like, right away."

"Would love that but why right away?" I slide the wine glass towards her across the marble countertop. "Holy shit, are you pregnant again?" I ask, pulling the wine glass back towards myself.

"I wasn't going to say anything yet."

"What? Why not?!" I run around the island and hug her.

"Well, I'm only 11 days DPO."

"Remind me what that stands for again?"

"Days past ovulation. So it's very early and could totally be a false positive."

"But probably not, right? You've been trying for six months now."

"And whenever I test early it's negative. But not this time. Anyway, I don't want to get my hopes up," she is smiling ear to ear.

"Might be too late for that," I say with a wink.

"Might be. So, you need to get knocked up a-s-a-p. Then we can be pregnant together!"

This is of course, our ultimate best friend dream. Having a whole year off work together and two adorable babies who we hope will also become best friends.

Nat and her husband Chad already have a 15-month-old son and they were hoping to have very close siblings. Instead, it's been six months of routine sex and negative tests. Chad even went on strike during month four, claiming that he felt used. I think Nat took my suggestion of some sex toys to heart though because I haven't heard of him denying her since.

I would never tell Nat this (because I'm ashamed to admit it even to myself), but a small part of me was relieved when her pregnancy tests came back negative. I didn't want to be left behind again. But this time I won't be because there's a ring in a velvet box promising me the future I've always dreamed of.

"Anyway, I don't know how we're even going to *afford* a second baby, we still have all that debt from the wedding and being laid off during COVID-19 didn't help either. Plus, Chad keeps pouring money into that *stupid* car of his – I swear, I should just set that relic on fire."

"You used to love that car when you first started dating."

"Oh god that was so long ago!"

"Well I don't think he's about to trade in a vintage Honda Del Sol for a mini-van."

"You're probably right," she laughs. "Ugh, now that it's here, I'm not even sure if I'm *ready* for a second baby. I know we've been trying for months but did I really think it through? Like how am I supposed to handle a newborn *and* a toddler?"

"Mmm, I wouldn't know," I say quietly, my mood changing instantly. This is a regular occurrence for me; melancholy sets in whenever I'm reminded about how I don't have a family and the uncertainty if I'll *ever* have one.

"Hey, don't do that," Nat says, laying a hand over mine. This is why a girl needs a best friend – someone who can read her instantly. Nat knows my dreams, my fears, all the fights with Darren as well as my own tormenting thoughts and anxieties. She recognizes the changes in my voice, my expression, and my energy. She can pick out what's wrong without asking because she knows everything there is to know about me. "You're going to be a mom. And soon! Hasn't Darren said that you'll start your family once you're married?"

"Yeah," I can feel a smile tugging at my lips, "he did say that."

"And now there's a ring!"

"Now there's a ring." My smile grows wider, a lot wider. "I'm going to have a baby!" Nat pulls me into a hug. "I wish my mom was still alive. She was supposed to walk me down the aisle," I whisper into her shoulder.

"She would be so happy for you. But she'd also try to control the wedding planning and she would be uncomfortably honest at the dress fittings." I laugh because I know Nat is right. "Remember that time when we were going out for your nineteenth birthday and she told you your dress was too slutty?"

"Yes! I remember texting you to tell you that and you replied that she was just being a prude and to send you a picture."

"And then I said I'm coming over, we're going shopping." We both laugh at the memory. It was a terrible dress, I don't know what I was thinking when I bought it. "Could you ever imagine when we were trolling the bars, picking up guys that we would end up here?" Nat asks wistfully. "I almost miss those days."

I cough with laughter, wine going up my nose. "What? You do not! We always met such LOSERS! Remember the ex-convict? My god; I can't believe you sexted him for *days*. I can't believe you even gave him your number in the first place!"

"Remember when I told my mom about him?"

"Oh yes and she gave you this big lecture about how you would never have sexual satisfaction from conjugal visits. It was hilarious."

"For you," Nat scoffs.

"For me."

"Remember your almost-tinder-date? The cunnilinguist," she clarifies when I give her a blank look.

"Oh yeah!"

"I still think you should have gone out with him. I mean yes, obviously a douchebag, but good oral skills should not be overlooked."

"I probably should have," I laugh.

"I think all men should take a cunnilingus course. Actually, probably a full degree in the female orgasm. The things I had to teach Chad when we met."

"I got lucky with Darren – he knew what he was doing."

"Oh yeah? Did you get rid of your vibrator then?"

"Don't be ridiculous," I scoff and we both double over with laughter.

When Nat leaves an hour later I begin my bedtime routine. I stare at myself in the mirror, flushed from the wine and laughter. I take my time brushing my teeth as I fantasize about Darren standing six feet tall in a navy suit at the alter. His black hair will be trimmed short and his clean-shaven face will wear a serious expression until he sees me. That's when he'll smile and his eyes will crinkle adorably.

Spitting out the minty toothpaste, I take in my own features; long blond hair and hazel eyes that are more brown than green. My cheeks are dotted with freckles and more will come out in the summertime with the sun. I smile at myself and take in my straight teeth and the dimple that I've always hated. I picture a white lace dress, my shoulders exposed by loose, off-the-shoulder sleeves and my hair in a fishtail braid with baby's breath. I'll wear a bold scarlet lipstick to match the flowers in my bouquet. I twirl, as if I'm actually wearing the dress and when I catch myself in the mirror, I see the hope shining bright in my eyes.

2

FEBRUARY 2023

Anna

I am anxiously counting down the days until Hawaii, giddy as I daydream about what Darren will say when he gets down on one knee. The frigid temperatures and days of endless snow make me that much more desperate to speed up time.

Today, the weather is no different. A blast of cold February air bites my cheeks as I push through the large glass doors of my office and I retreat further into the swaddle of my scarf. I find myself missing the early days of the COVID-19 pandemic. During lockdown I could work remotely and I'd watch the snow fall from inside my cozy house. I had a thick blanket, my laptop and I rarely changed out of my pyjamas. But with this longing for work-from-home days comes a wave of guilt because the pandemic took what mattered most from me – my mom. I lost her to the virus that first pandemic summer; I wasn't even allowed to say goodbye, not really – FaceTime doesn't count. I stamp my feet as I wait at the crosswalk in an attempt to shake the cold and the painful memories that threaten to surface.

My co-worker Gabby and I are heading out to grab some lunch after a long morning of back-to-back meetings. We walk a few blocks between the tall skyscrapers of downtown Toronto. Even after years of working downtown, I still marvel at the old architecture of these buildings and the historic detail of the early 1900's. With my eyes to the sky I miss a puddle and instantly the toes of my suede wedge boots become soaked with grey slush. Fuck. Thankfully Chipotle is just across the street offering imminent warmth.

"Do you want kids?" Gabby asks me once we sit down with our burrito bowls and unwrap ourselves from the layers of winter clothing. I don't even try to answer because I can tell this is a rhetorical question and the beginning of one of her rants. Sure enough, she digs in right away. "I don't understand why people have kids. Like at all. They ruin your life, you can't go out, you can't sleep in, they require so much attention and they have so many activities – not to mention you're forced to buy a minivan," she shudders at the thought.

"K, I want kids, but you'll never catch me driving a minivan."

"Uh huh," she says like she doesn't believe it. "I was at my sister's place on the weekend, she's got a three-year-old, an eleven-month-old and…! She's pregnant! Again! She was supposed to go back to work in like one month. Anna, you should have seen her – her eyes had this pleading look like she's been kidnapped and needs to be saved but if she says anything her captors will kill us both."

"It couldn't have been that bad."

"The three-year-old took off his poopy diaper and stuck his

hand in it and then we literally chased him around the house, up and down the stairs, through every room as he dragged his shitty, little, shit-covered hand along the walls. It was like a TV show. In the end, I had to pin him down on the kitchen floor while she cleaned his hands and put another diaper on him."

"Maybe it was an off day?"

"Last weekend he threw himself face first into the coffee table and they were at the ER until two am."

"Oh my god, is he ok?"

"Oh yeah, he's fine," she waves me off like this is a regular occurrence, "and then she asks me what I did on the weekend. What was I supposed to say? Nick and I took molly and danced our asses off at Rebel until four in the morning but I didn't want to rub it in. So I lied and told her we fell asleep on the couch watching Netflix. Turns out she was more jealous of the Netflix and chill, and that's just sad, " Gabby says through a mouthful of burrito. "I'm never having kids."

I look down at my lunch to hide the upward curve of my lips. For the first time in a long time I feel hope instead of tearful anxiety when the topic of *having kids* comes up. For the past couple of years, I could barely stomach talking about kids (which is a really hard conversation to avoid as you head from your twenties to your thirties). Each conversation was a stark reminder that Darren and I had totally different timelines. But now there's a velvet box and a blinking diamond to set my worries to rest.

3

FEBRUARY 2023

Anna

I've been riding a high ever since I found the ring, holding the pleasurable secret of my new future inside. Darren has caught me smiling to myself a few times now and he asks me what I'm so happy about but I just smile wider and say *oh nothing*. But he does manage to pop the bubble of bliss eventually.

On a Thursday night, while Darren is in the basement playing Xbox, I call Nat to complain about him. He has his headphones on and he's shouting military commands at his friends but even still, I take the precaution of heading to the top floor bathroom before dialing.

The first thing I say when Nat answers the phone is, "I hate men."

She's pretty used to this routine by now. "Uh huh, what happened now?"

"He can be SO rude. And then so oblivious."

"Well, men are idiots, it's been scientifically proven. Do you have any more specifics?"

"He asked me why I'm watching trash TV again. Again? Like what the fuck; why are you playing your stupid videogame, again? "

"Rude. What were you watching?"

"Love Is Blind. And Nick and Danielle were having this ridiculous fight-"

"STOP RIGHT THERE. I'm not caught up. I love that show. But, I mean, it is kind of trashy reality TV."

"Whose side are you on anyway?"

Nat ignores my question completely. "So are you giving Darren the silent treatment?"

"Yeah, mostly. I did ask him about pizza toppings but I wasn't friendly about it and I took all the good pieces."

"Naturally. You can't let him off the hook that easy."

"I don't think he even realizes that I'm mad."

"Ugh, men. So, are you getting excited for your trip?"

"Yeah, but I'm a little nervous too."

"About the proposal?"

"No, just travelling in general. It will be our first trip since the pandemic. What if something goes wrong?"

"What would go wrong?"

"I don't know, what if there's another lockdown?"

"I don't think you have to worry about that. It's been more than a year since the last lockdown. Why would they do it again? Everyone's already had COVID; you don't even have to isolate anymore."

"I know but what about new variants and stuff?"

"I wouldn't worry. We've got our vaccines and our politicians are too slow to ever do anything anyway. Nothing is going to happen that we don't see coming."

"Yeah, I guess you're right."

"I'm sure it will feel weird to travel now but just enjoy it. You're so lucky you get to go somewhere; I can't even take my kid to a freakin' grocery store much less on a plane. Oh crap, Chad's calling me, I've got to go."

"No problem, I'll talk to you later."

"It's all going to be ok," she says quickly before hanging up.

4

MARCH 2023

Anna

I'm sweating beneath my down winter coat despite the negative temperatures as I run down Queen St, weaving in between impeccably dressed professionals. When I first started working in Toronto I was surprised (and envious) over just how well dressed everyone was. In an effort to fit in, I purchased Airpods, overpriced blouses from Aritzia and a camel-coloured, wool trench coat with my first paycheque. It didn't take me long to switch back to jeans and plain t-shirts and a warm, puffy coat. Commuting two hours every day requires comfort over fashion.

I've just finished my last day of work before our trip to Hawaii and unfortunately I got caught in a last-minute call that went past 5pm. Now I've got less than ten minutes to get to my salon that is fifteen minutes away for my first ever Brazilian wax.

My stomach is turning over with nerves as I slow to a power walk and think about how I'll have to strip from the waist down.

I've had bikini waxes before but that's easy, just move the underwear here, ok there, done. I'm half hoping that I'll be too late and they won't be able to take me.

My Airpods stop playing Mumford And Sons and announce an incoming call. I already know it's Nat before Siri says her name robotically, and I already know why she's calling – because she knows I want to chicken out. I tap my headphones to answer the call and without even saying hello, I launch into, "Nat, she's going to see my vag! A total stranger, under fluorescent lights!"

"Would you rather it be someone you know?"

"Of course not!"

"Exactly. And you know she's going to be seeing more than that, right? Between the cheeks, if you know what I mean."

"Oh god, why did I book this?"

"Because the last time you tried to wax yourself you ripped some skin off."

"Well, yeah, that was bad. But that doesn't mean I need some stranger between my cheeks. I could just get a regular bikini wax."

"But it's Hawaii! And your engagement! Live a little."

"Ugh! K, I just got to the salon, I'll text you after."

"Send pics!"

"Wha—"

"Just kidding! Obvi. Go," she says with a laugh as she hangs up the call. I take in my surroundings as I push through the glass doors of the high-end salon. Everything is white and clean and glossy which puts me a little at ease.

Sadly the feeling doesn't last and I feel incredibly awkward as I lie on the table with my knees open. She's asking me all kinds of questions about myself and it's just like when the doctor makes small talk during a pap smear; *how was your day, are you still working at the same place, oh your cervix is being a little shy today.* Like stop, please stop, so I can just pretend that I don't exist anymore.

She's very professional and just being friendly but damn – it's awkward. I leave a big tip for her in the hopes that she doesn't go home and tell her friends about my vag. Not that I think my vag is weird or noteworthy but like, I don't know. Someone's going to ask her about her day, right?

By the time I exit the salon I have to run again just to catch the last commuter train home. I only just make it so of course there are no seats left and I'm forced to stand in the aisle, shoulder to shoulder with strangers. I pull a blue, crumpled facemask from my coat pocket and put it on. I'm still uncomfortable being in a crowd of strangers this tight. Even though mask mandates were removed last year, it is still somewhat common to see people wearing them on the GO train and the subway.

The news barely mentions COVID-19 anymore but I still feel anxious about it in large crowds. I think it's harder for those who have lost someone to the virus. I often wonder if the people around me wearing masks have lost a loved one too. Sometimes I want to ask them so that I can share the pain of losing my mom with someone who truly understands it, but I never do.

Losing her was the worst thing to happen to me. I remember when we lost my grandma and my mom told me that no matter how old you are, you always need your mom. I was young then, maybe eleven, so it didn't hit home like it does now. And it really hits. Hard. I still need her, maybe now more than ever.

My dad left before my second birthday and my mom raised me all on her own. We were always close when I was growing up and closer still when I was older. We talked every single day – until the day she went into the hospital. Not hearing her voice was like a huge hole in my life. A black hole. It started to suck everything in and tried to suck me in too.

It was months before I slept through the night again. As soon as she was admitted, I started having trouble sleeping. I'd wake up in the middle of the night, my skin clammy with sweat and my clothes soaked. My heart would race with panic and my breathing would come in short gasps. If it wasn't for Darren, waking with me and calming me down, I might never have slept again.

Just when things seemed to be getting better, she died. She had come off of the ventilator a week before and everyone told us she was on the mend. Fifty-nine with no underlying conditions, the doctors were taken by surprise. But everyone was still learning just what the virus could do at that point. I had talked to her the day before, her nurse helping her to FaceTime me. I could tell that her throat was still sore from the ventilator by the rasp in her voice so I did most of the talking. She even smiled when I told her that Darren had decorated our dining room to make it feel like our favourite restaurant and took me 'out to dinner' to give me a date night despite lockdown restrictions.

The next day when the doctor called me, I answered with a casualness and an ease; I was expecting another positive update. Instead, he told me that she was gone. It didn't matter how much I loved her or how badly I still needed her, the virus took her and I wasn't going to get her back.

My nightly panic attacks grew more severe and my days were spent on the couch in a depression. I subscribed to HGTV so that I could watch my mom's favourite shows and I spent weeks on the couch doing just that.

It was more than grief and at a time that everything was closed under provincial lockdown orders, I had no outlets to deal with my feelings. I sank deeper into my depression and I felt incapable of anything. My bereavement leave ended but I didn't get off the couch, didn't turn off the TV. Darren took over then, calling doctors and counsellors and holding my hand through Zoom appointments. Thanks to Darren, I got the help I needed and things started to improve. They weren't back to normal, but they were better and whenever he noticed my bottom lip trembling with tears, he would ask me to share a favourite memory of my mom. The tears would still fall but I would be smiling too.

Nat and her endless string of supportive, hilarious, or reminiscent texts was another reason I didn't get sucked into that black hole. My phone chimes now with a text from her, probably wanting to know how my vag looks, and I'm pulled from my thoughts of the pandemic.

N: Well? 🐱

A: I did it! kept a landing strip tho 🛫

N: this is going to be a good week for you 🍆 🐚

N: 😌😌

N: so how awkward was it?

A:

A: she had a spotlight and everything 😂 not even Darren's seen it like that before.

N: lmfao 😄

A: yeah. it looks good tho!

N: 👍

I hear someone snort with laughter behind me and I turn

around to find a tall guy in a flashy suit reading my texts over my shoulder. OH GOD! He at least has the decency to blush when he notices that I've caught him. When the doors open at the next station he rushes out with the rest of the crowd. I watch out the window as the mass of exiting passengers burst into a sprint the moment they hit the pavement, heading in all different directions. It's like a very disorganized track and field event. Now that the train has emptied a good portion of its passengers, I head upstairs to find a seat in the quiet section, hoping that I can nap the rest of the way home.

It's after 7pm when my train finally pulls into the Hamilton GO station and I walk the last few blocks home. We live in a quiet neighbourhood in the downtown core that is full of old churches and one-hundred-year-old homes. Some are falling apart but most are lovingly restored. Tonight, the sky is dark and heavy with clouds and a light snowfall. The city is beautiful when it's lightly dusted with snow but I miss summer, when the sun sinks behind the gothic spires of the cathedrals and casts dark shadows across the city.

I'm cold and exhausted by the time I stand in front of our own home. It's on its way to being lovingly restored but we bought it during COVID when we both worked from home and had more time to invest in renovations. Now we just shut the pocket doors on our dining room to hide the piles of lumber and flooring and paint cans.

When I walk in the house I'm hit with the smell of chicken curry and I'm positive that it's from my favourite take-out spot.

"Do I smell Indian food from the Shehnai or am I hallucinating?"

"Your nose never lies, Anna."

"Oh, you're a life saver." I walk up behind Darren at the

kitchen sink and hug him from behind. He cranes his neck around to give me a kiss.

"How was your day? How was the wax?" He wiggles his eyebrows suggestively. I laugh as he hands me a bowl.

"You'll see later," I give him a suggestive wink as I sit down at the kitchen island. I'm lying, he's not going to see it tonight – I fully intend to fall asleep the moment I've finished packing.

I start into my food right away – usually I would wait for Darren to sit down next to me before I start eating but not tonight, tonight I practically inhale my food. I didn't have time to eat lunch today and I'm starving. Plus getting all the hair ripped from your most sensitive body parts builds an appetite. I half-listen to Darren as he talks about his workday as a game developer. He's saying something about a particular line of code and how he was stuck on it for hours only to find a semi-colon was missing at the end. I smile and nod but really I'm thinking about all the things I need to pack. I haven't even gotten our suitcases out of the storage room yet and I know they're buried right at the bottom.

After dinner I dig them out and lug both mine and Darren's up to the bedroom while he does the dishes. I start throwing clothes into my suitcase haphazardly. I think of the 4am alarm I've set and of how badly I just want to fall face first into our bed right now but I've got to wear *something* in Hawaii. I grab sundresses and sandals along with underwear and tank tops. I waiver over my favourite jean shorts that I haven't worn in forever because every time I put them on I wonder if I'm too old to wear short-shorts and I take them off not wanting to find out. Thirty-two isn't that old, right? Fuck it, I throw them in and then swap out my one-piece bathing suit for the new bikini I bought even though I haven't exactly met my pre-vacation goal weight. I figure there's no way I can hate my body when it's sun-kissed by the Hawaiian sun and sporting a new diamond ring.

5

MARCH 2023

Anna

My alarm goes off at 4am as expected but I snooze it twice before eventually getting out of bed and pushing Darren out with me. I feel as though I've barely slept. I'm hoping with the long flight from Toronto to Honolulu that I will have plenty of time to catch up. From there we have a short connecting flight to the island of Kauai and then we will officially be in paradise.

As I gather my suitcase, purse and carry-on at the door, I decide that it's too many bags. I don't want to carry a purse and a carry-on so I migrate only the essentials into the carry-on bag. I dig through the huge pile of receipts in my purse to find what I need: wallet; Airpods; I can forget the tampons thank god; three colours of lipstick; birth control pills –

"Anna!" Darren shouts down the stairs, making me jump and I drop everything in my hand. My pills and lipsticks go skidding under the couch.

"WHAT?!"

"Where is my bathing suit?"

"Huh?" I'm on my hands and knees reaching under the couch trying to find my things but all I feel are crumbs and hairballs. Gross.

"WHERE IS MY BATHING SUIT?" He shouts down the stairs, enunciating each word slowly. "I can't find it; did you wash it? Where did you put it?"

"Are you telling me you're not finished PACKING?!" Silence. "DARREN! We have to *leave* in 20 minutes!"

"Can you just come help me? Please?"

"UGH!" I still haven't found my pills or my lipsticks; I'll have to move the couch. I abandon it for now and stomp up the stairs to help Darren. Thirty minutes later, we run down the stairs with his suitcase and I'm frazzled because we're already late. I stuff my feet into a pair of UGGs, grab my bags and shove Darren out the door.

What feels like years later (but it's really only nineteen hours) we are lying in a comfy, king-sized bed, drained from the day's travel. It was late afternoon when we flew into Honolulu and the sun was just starting to sink. By the time we landed on Kauai, the sun had fully set and we drove beneath a starry sky to our Airbnb.

I was happy to discover that the place we booked was even nicer than in the photos. Our host Lisa was waiting for us on the porch with Mai-Tai's when we arrived and she lead us around the side of the house, down a winding path lined on either side by a lush garden to the private coach house that is our suite. Two French doors with gauzy curtains opened into a big room that is dominated by a mural of the ocean on the far wall behind the commanding king-size bed. There's a sofa that looks so comfy one could sink into it and never come out, a refinished antique dresser sits opposite the bed and the ensuite bathroom is breathtaking. It's all marble with a glass shower and a giant soaker tub. Not to be forgotten and probably my favourite feature is the outdoor garden shower. A stone path lined with green, frondy plants, leads to a concrete pad. Above, a massive rainfall shower head pokes out of the concrete wall that is carved with Polynesian designs. There are flowers of every colour planted around the shower base. The whole thing is enclosed by a tall, wood privacy fence. Perfect for engagement sex? I think so.

Lisa left us to unpack and we retired early. Darren is already asleep next to me but I'm wide awake. When we went to bed, we left the terrace doors open and the scents and sounds of the garden drift in on the soft ocean breeze. I'm tickled by the sweet smell of the plumeria trees and if I listen hard enough, I can hear the waves washing against the beach only half a kilometer away. The peacefulness is only slightly dampened by Darren's snores.

Despite my exhaustion, I can't seem to fall asleep. I have this anxious feeling that I've forgotten something at home but I can't think of what it would be. I also can't sleep for all my excitement – Darren and I have dreamed of coming to Hawaii for a long time; not to mention, I can't wait for him to propose.

Well, if I can't sleep, I'm going to save more wedding ideas to my Pinterest board. I roll out from under Darren's arm that is flung across my middle and reach for my phone that's on the nightstand. The light of the screen blinds me for a moment but then my eyes adjust. I open my Pinterest app and start scrolling through the endless photos of wedding dresses, décor and flower arrangements. Other than the venue, I might have the entire wedding already planned and the ring isn't even on my finger yet. I've spent the past few weeks alternating between Pinterest wedding board building and adding mine and Darren's photos to a baby generator app to see what our kids would look like. It was multiple tries and a few worries before I realized that the app purposely creates ugly babies.

"What's that light," Darren asks groggily.

"Oh, nothing, it's just my phone." I quickly drop it facedown on the bedside table before he can see my wedding board. I don't want him to know I know. I roll over to face him and he smiles and kisses me on the nose. "We're in Hawaii," I whisper, shimmying my body even closer to his.

He closes his eyes and smiles wider, "yup. Paradise."

"Don't go back to sleep," I say.

"Mmmm, I'm not. Not asleep."

"You are."

"Am not."

"Wake up," I whisper as I roll on top of him, I kiss him tenderly on the lips and he sighs in pleasure. I kiss the side of his mouth, his chin, his neck, the tender spot behind his ear; I take his earlobe between my teeth and slide my tongue along the soft skin. Another sigh escapes him. He stares into my eyes as his hands move to cup my ass before slowly sliding up the length of my body to cup my breasts. He pinches my nipples lightly between thumb and forefinger and a slow wave of pleasure snakes up my spine. His lips are on my neck and he's hard between my thighs. Suddenly wide awake, Darren wraps his arm around me and deftly rolls us over so he is on top. Now it's my turn to sigh. I fall into the deep down of the pillows and he lifts my thin tank top and his mouth finds my nipples, his tongue darting out to taste and flick the firm buds. A deep noise, somewhere between a moan and growl, starts in his throat and in an instant the rest of our clothes are gone.

DARREN

I kiss Anna tenderly as I gently roll off of her, spent and satisfied. She whispers, "I really am in paradise," a smug smile on her lips as she snuggles under my arm. I could stay just like this forever but I think of the diamond ring in my suitcase. I've had it for months knowing that I wanted to propose in Hawaii. I thought that I would wait for the right dinner or the right sunset but this moment right here feels like the right moment.

"Don't go back to sleep," I say, repeating her words from earlier as I drag myself out of bed.

"Mmm, but I'm so tired."

Her eyes are glazed and droopy with sleep so I have no time to bother with clothes. I run over to my suitcase and shove my hand deep into the front pocket. For a second I can't locate the ring box and I start having heart palpitations but then my fingertips feel the soft, crushed velvet. The zipper bites my arm as I pull it out of the suitcase and race back over to the bed. Anna looks dreamy, the white sheets draped casually over her, her blond hair splayed across the pillow. I love how her carefully straightened hair has reverted back to its natural wave in the humidity.

"Anna, wake up."

"I'm awake," she mumbles without opening her eyes. I slip back under the sheets, drape it around my waist for some kind of modesty, as I kneel before her. The box creaks loudly as I open it. Her lips curl up in a smile exposing that beautiful dimple I love so much, before she even opens her eyes. When she sees the ring her eyes start to well with tears and with a nervous laugh, I take the ring out and slip it onto her third finger. As she lays there, she closes her eyes again in an attempt to cage her tears but two escape, marking a trail to her mouth. I kiss her and taste their salt. "Yes," she whispers against my lips.

"I didn't ask you anything yet," I laugh and she joins me. She opens her eyes again and they're brimming. She lets the tears fall unhindered. I want to tell her what she means to me, what she's always meant. I want to tell about the life we'll lead and the happiness we'll find but I don't know how to put it all into words so I just say, "I love you, Anna. Will you marry me?"

"You know I will," she grabs my face and pulls my mouth to hers for a kiss and I fall on top of her into the softness of the pillows. She stretches her body against the length of mine and soon the sheets are no longer between us; there's nothing between us.

6

MARCH 2023

Anna

I wake before Darren and pad quietly around the room, slipping into one of my casual sundresses and then tip-toeing out the terrace doors. I walk barefoot into the garden. Smiling up at the sun, it feels like I might never wear a sad expression again. I stare down at my ring, at the sun refracting off of the emerald cut diamond. I feel worth something; worth someone; my future stretching ahead of me. I wish I didn't put so much worth in a ring (or lack thereof) but our society still relies on rings and weddings to mark the depth of a couple's commitment. And now I know how committed Darren is.

I bite my smile, twisting the new ring around my finger. I plop down into the colourful hammock strung between the garden trees and pull out my phone to text Nat.

A: You never told me that engaged sex was better than regular sex!! 💍

N: AH!!! OMG! So it's official!! Congrats babe!

N: No of course I didn't tell you that, poor Darren already had enough pressure from you to propose 😜

A: lol

A: it was like so perfect, Nat. so fucking perfect 🤩

N: amazing! Can't wait to hear all the details

A: so if engagement sex is that good, how's the wedding sex?

N: it's all downhill from here girl, enjoy it while you got it 😆

A: 😬

A: how are you doing? 🍞

N: 🤢

A: Oh no!

N: toast with butter is like the only thing I can keep down 🤮

N: why do I have to have morning sickness? Isn't that like so 1990's?

A: that doesn't even make sense.

N: it's 2023 – shouldn't they have drugs for this by now?

A: pretty sure they do.

N: but you have to be like super duper pukey to get them, trust me, I asked.

A: lol of course, did your midwife tell you to woman-up?

N: no

A: well she should have 😏

"Anna?" I hear Darren call through the open terrace doors.

"Out here!" I shout. I struggle to escape from the low hammock, nearly dumping myself in the process. I text Nat a quick TTYL and slip my phone into my dress pocket.

Darren walks up to me, rubbing his eyes. He's wearing nothing but boxers and I can't help staring at his body. Five years together has done nothing to dull my attraction to him.

His body is slim and toned but not overly defined. He goes to the gym semi-regularly and it gives him a mild definition that lets you know he takes care of himself without being obsessed with his appearance. The hair on his chest is dark and sparse, a thin trail down his torso.

He pulls me into his arms and I burrow my face into his neck, breathing in the sandalwood scent of him. He takes my left hand and tenderly twists the new ring around my finger, "so it wasn't a dream?"

"It's the best dream. Our life is a dream."

Suddenly Lisa rounds the corner and comes into view just as I contemplate pulling Darren back into our room and spending the whole day in bed.

"Oh good, you're already up. I hope you slept well," her smile is wide and open.

"That bed is amazing," I say, returning Lisa's smile.

"Great, well breakfast is ready for you in the kitchen."

"Oh, perfect!"

Darren waits behind me until Lisa heads back toward the house and then he jogs back to our suite to get dressed. I follow Lisa back to the main house and in the open concept kitchen I find the island laden with plates of fresh cut fruit, bacon and eggs of all forms.

"Well, this looks amazing," I say and take a bite of pineapple. My body sags with pleasure as the sweet juice fills my mouth. "Oh my god! This is the best pineapple I've ever eaten!"

"Everything tastes sweeter in Hawaii. So," Lisa says, pulling up a stool and spearing a piece of watermelon with a fork, "I didn't notice that ring on your finger last night."

I smile shyly and play with the ring, "it's new."

"It's beautiful."

"Thanks."

"Do you have a date in mind?"

"I've always dreamed of a fall wedding, capture the colour of the leaves."

"Gorgeous. So tell me, how did you and Darren meet?"

I laugh, "we met the same way everyone meets these days – on a dating app."

I can't contain my smile as I dwell on the memory of meeting Darren. We talked for a couple of weeks on Tinder before meeting up at a busy pub in downtown Hamilton on a Saturday night. We talked so much we barely finished one drink each in three hours. It was a great date which is almost worst than a bad date because then you're the one whose likely getting ghosted. But Darren didn't really get the chance (not that he would have taken it, he promises).

The day after our date, Nat called me and tried to convince me that going out on a Sunday night was a good idea.

"Hey, let's go to open mic night at the Baltimore House," she said as soon as I answered the phone.

"What? But it's Sunday, I'm about to put on track pants."

"Jeez, what are you, 30?"

"Um, you know I'm only 27. You're the old one."

"Oh yes, 27 and a half is ancient. Come on, we're not old yet! And anyway, it starts at 7pm. Surely you can handle that?"

"If I go you have to do something for me."

"Yes, yes, anything."

"You have to ask out the bartender. I'm tired of watching you drool over him."

"Anything but that."

"I know you like him."

"I do not."

"You do."

"I can't date a guy with a mustache. It's against my policy."

"I bet you any money if you leaned across that bar with a little cleavage and said you love clean shaven men, it would be gone the next day."

"HA! I'm not that kind of hussy."

"Uh-huh."

"If I was, I don't think he would shave it anyway. Do you see how well groomed it is? He's probably so attached to it. Hipsters these days." I don't bring up her over-sized glasses or penchant for plaid when she says this.

"Well, we will see."

"So, you'll be there?"

"While you're asking him out? I wouldn't miss it. See you at 7."

"I'm not goi---" but I had already hung up.

I arrived at Baltimore House a few hours later, walking up the few steps into the non-descript brick building. Divided into two rooms, one of them was like your grandma's living room. There were crushed velvet couches and small, spindly coffee tables and Tiffany lamps. The other room was lined with old church pews facing each other over wooden tables. The pews were heavily defaced with graffiti – mostly penises and poems about penises – and there were strange pictures of Jesus everywhere. Tripadvisor might call it a hidden gem. Or offensive.

The bartender that Nat was crushing on so hard was the exact depiction of a hipster. They should have a picture of him on UrbanDictonary.com under "Hipster". Picture black-framed glasses, suspenders, bowtie, and waxed mustache curled at the corners.

I walked up to the bar and ordered two Somersby's for us and waited for Nat who was always late. The band had already started up in the other room by the time she arrived and we grabbed our drinks and ducked our heads as we shuffled in front of the crowd to the only available table left – an antique table that was more the size of a night table and two chairs so small you'd think they were made for a kindergartener. We sat side by side on the far side of the table so that we could both see the band. I was so close to the guitar player that I was worried he might elbow me in the head so I made Nat scooch over further. When I was finally situated, I looked up at the band and got quite the surprise. It was Darren, my great date from the night before. He did say something about a band, but I just figured it was him and his buddies playing classic rock in someone's garage while they drank.

Darren's band was covering Aerosmith's I Don't Want To Miss A Thing which is a song that everyone ever knows so I could tell immediately when Darren fumbled the cords – he had just laid eyes on me as well. His band mates were glaring at him viciously, and he dropped his eyes to his fingers, chiseled jaw clenched as he tried to course correct.

I looked back and forth between Nat and Darren.

"Guitar player is hot, isn't he?" She shouted at me. I looked back at Darren and he was looking at us with a stricken expression. He heard her. I pulled out my phone and texted Nat instead of embarrassed myself out loud.

She was nodding her head to the music and ignoring her phone so I had to poke her in the arm. "Ow!," she rubbed her bicep.

I pointed to her phone and she picked it up and read my text.

A: Omg it's Darren!

N: Huh? Who's Darren?

A: My Tinder date! From yesterday!

N: Omg where?

A: The guitar player!

N: The hot one?

A: there's only one...

N: Oh. My. God. Did you know he would be here? Are we stalking him???

A: You invited me, remember?

N: Oh right 😂

N: he's hot though 😌 🍆

A: put it back in your pants, Nat! He's mine lol but yes, totally hot 🔥

N: I think he heard me when I shouted it.

A: Definitely

N: 🙈

N: He looks like he would be good in bed. You should find out.

A: Hmm, I should. Just for purely scientific reasons

N: science in the bedroom. Sexy.

I quickly jumped to my browser to look up sex emojis because at 27 I was no longer fluent in the perverted lingo of the youth.

A: 👉 👌

A: 🍑 🍆 💦

A: 🌮 🍒 💦

I waited for Nat's response which would no doubt be obscene and hilarious but no response came – very weird because Nat loves to carry on convos in only emojis. I gave her a quizzical look across the table and she just looked at me like what?. I

checked my phone. Oh god, oh god, oh god. I sent those last messages to Darren. OH GOD. Christ, that must have happened when I was flipping between Google and my texts.

At the realization, I slammed my head down on the table in over-the-top exasperation. This caused a chain reaction. Our drinks slid off the table, drenching both myself and Nat. She jumped up in sudden shock which knocked over our table into Darren, who was somehow still strumming out Aerosmith (now Walk This Way). He ended up falling into the drum set and every set of eyes in the bar was on Nat and I.

I ran over to Darren to give him a hand up but I ended up tripping over his amp cord and falling on top of him instead. His head jerked back with the force and hit the symbol of the drum set.

I'm sure I had a mortified look on my face and my clothes were soaked with booze. I remember Darren was looking extremely embarrassed and then out of nowhere, he unceremoniously snorted with laughter.

"Is this our meet cute moment then?" He asked me, a smile playing at his lips.

"I guess so," I smiled and courageously planted my lips on his, kissing him deeply in front of the whole bar. We received whoops and cheers from everyone but his bandmates.

While we made out on the floor, the bartender wrestled the microphone from the lead singer, "ah, Chad, come on, just let us finish our set," the singer said as they had a bit of a tug of war over the mic. Chad finally got it away from him and said "give it up for The Hot Carls. Our next band will be up momentarily." And a group of goths in the back corner started scrambling and chugging their drinks.

I give Lisa the full story and she's bubbling with laughter by the end of it. "That's an amazing story!" Lisa laughs, "but now that I know how you two ended up together, I have to ask – did Nat ask out the bartender?"

"She married him!"

"No way! Really? That makes it even better."

Darren walks into the kitchen fully dressed and squeezes my shoulder as he walks past me towards the food.

"I hear you're quite the rockstar," Lisa says to Darren.

"Famous even," he jokes, taking in the breakfast spread. "Lisa, this looks amazing." He turns to me and asks, "do I have time to eat some of this before we go?"

"If you hurry. I want to get to the beach early."

Darren eats quickly but when we get to the beach it's already packed, just shy of 10am. I've seen the ocean before but never like this. It is absolutely breathtaking here in Hawaii. The shore isn't a straight line but curves like a woman's body. I grab Darren's hand and pull him to the water's edge to tip my toes in and admire the azure blue of the water, the darker turquoise of the coral beneath and the silvery dart of small fish. I watch the waves wash against the sand, a white bubbly froth outlining each wave as it creeps up the sand. Turning around, we survey the beach. Families and couples and friends and surfers have all carved out their own spots on the sand. Tourists and locals alike are friendly, offering smiles and small talk about the surroundings as we walk along the beach, looking for our spot. We find a place of our own and lay out a blanket. I step out of my shorts and shirt and lay down in my bikini, ready to soak up some sun.

Darren falls asleep almost immediately under the hot morning sun, a Toronto Blue Jays cap covering his eyes. I worry about him burning but he already waved off my offer of sunscreen. His olive skin from Italian ancestry doesn't burn like mine he says. I apply my own and then lie next to him with my book but I can't concentrate on the words. Instead, I'm listening to the conversations of others around me, taking in the minutia of their days, the bickering between couples, and the secrets between friends. When the sun becomes too hot for me, I walk down to the water's edge and walk in up to my thighs.

I marvel in the feeling of the sand between my toes, being sucked back by the ocean like it's not willing to share. I walk along the shore, ankle deep in the warm water and I notice how the palm trees grow away from the water, pushed and molded by the strong winds.

Drawing my eyes away from the trees, I survey the people around me and I can't help but notice that there's more ass on display than in an episode of Game of Thrones. No one informed me that thong bathing suits were trendy. I try not to compare myself to the perfect, tanned bodies around me but it feels impossible. My extra weight seems to hang heavier on my frame as I size them up. I try to remind myself that other women might look at me and wish they had my body. It's all subjective, we all want what we don't have. I think back to myself ten years and thirty pounds ago. I wasn't even happy with my body then, if only I could have known how much I'd long for that body now.

DARREN

I wake from my nap when Anna flops down beside me, cool drops of saltwater landing on my arm. She lifts my hat off of my face to give me a kiss. Her long blond hair is messy and tangled from the ocean breeze.

"How's the water?" I ask.

"Glorious. I was actually thinking that I might want to try surfing," she says.

"Go for it."

"Want to come?"

"Nah, I'd rather watch," I say and I mean it. I love watching her when she's learning something new. The mix of excitement and determination and pride on her face is always a turn on.

She runs over to the surf shop in the middle of the beach and within 10 minutes she's lying on a board and a teenage instructor hovering over her. She lies prone on the surfboard in the sand and then pops up to a crouch with a quick jump. Within the hour she's riding a tiny wave to shore. She waves to me, a smile of pride bringing out that dimple again but before she can reach the shore her arms start pinwheeling and she goes down with a splash.

After another hour or so, Anna comes back to me positively glowing. I want to kiss every dewy droplet of water on her skin but when I suggest we go back to the house, she suggests tacos instead. There's a small taco stand across the street from the beach so we grab a couple and come back to our spot. We sit crossed legged in the sand, laughing at each other for the different coloured sauces dripping down our chins and arms as the tacos fall apart in our hands and mouths. When we kiss, I taste pineapples and habaneros on her tongue.

Anna

We stay at the beach until the sun begins to set and my

skin feels tender with what is sure to be a wicked sunburn. We drive slowly back to the Airbnb with the windows down and the ocean breeze cooling our skin. We laugh our way into the garden shower where we wash our sticky bodies free of salt, sweat and hot sauce. Beneath the cascade of cool water Darren kisses every new freckle that's been exposed by the Hawaiian sun. He kneels on the stones, lifting my right foot to rest on his shoulder and he kisses me until the waves crash over me again and again.

7

MARCH 2023

DARREN

It's day four of our vacation and Anna convinced me to trade in the beaches of Kauai for the rainforests. I agreed without fully knowing what I was getting into.

Anna is in front of me, climbing the steep incline of the trail easily while I struggle a few meters behind her. I might go to the gym but I lift weights and avoid all cardio. Anna likes to run on the weekends so her lungs are more equipped for this than mine. When I finally crest the hill she's standing at the lookout, hands on her hips and eyes surveying the rugged coastline below us. She's dropped her small backpack to the ground and I can see thin strips of pale skin left behind by her bikini straps against the tender pink of her sunburn. I want to trace those pale lines with my tongue, follow them beneath her sports bra and the waistband of her leggings. But there's no time for fooling around as there's another group of hikers close behind us on the trail.

Instead, I quickly pull out my phone and snap a picture of Anna standing there, looking over the ocean.

"Look at this view!" She says as she spins around to see me.

"It's beautiful," I wheeze, looking right at her. I'm still not close enough to the edge to see much. Anna smiles and grabs my hand, pulling me to her for a kiss. She smells like sunscreen.

"I need to sit," she says, "my legs are shaking." She perches on a large boulder amidst the emerald green vegetation. There are flowers blooming all around us, the blooms featuring all the colours of the sunset. I snap another picture of her when she isn't looking. I walk closer to the edge and take in the sweeping view of the ocean. When I turn back to Anna a few minutes later, I notice a subtle shift in her the set of her shoulders, like a weight has been added.

"Are you thinking about your Mom?" I ask, already knowing the answer.

"Yeah, when we took that hiking trip in Ireland."

"And she totally outpaced you?"

Anna laughs, "hey, she ran marathons and I was a college student surviving on vodka and Delissio pizza. It was hardly a fair match-up."

"I'm so glad I met you after you learned to cook," I say sarcastically and she laughs. She still has no clue how to cook. "What's your favourite memory with your mom from that trip?"

"Probably when she got drunk in the Dublin pub and convinced the band to let her play the fiddle for one song."

"Your mom was such a lightweight," I laugh.

"Such a lightweight! And a terrible violin player."

"Oh, I'm aware. Remember when she played for my parents one Christmas?"

"Oh god. You did warn me that they shouldn't meet. I wish I had listened," Anna jokes.

"Her and my mom still became best friends so it all worked out."

"I died a little when she added her to Facebook. Before they'd even met!"

"I bet they've already planned our wedding," I joke.

"Probably." A sadness has creeped into her voice. "I wish she was going to be there"

"Me too," I say as Anna looks back out to the ocean.

"Darren, look! I think those are dolphins!" Anna exclaims, pointing down towards the water.

"Cool." We watch them swim and play along the craggy coastline for another minute until we are joined by more hikers who have reached the lookout. Holding hands, we turn back to the trail and make our way slowly back to the car, any thoughts of parents left behind us like footprints.

Anna

After a full day of hiking yesterday and an evening of scratching incessantly at mosquito bites, Darren and I decide to spend today at the beach. We look at Google Maps and find a beach that we haven't explored yet – we'll never see them all as there's too many to discover but I wish we could – at this point I never want to go home.

Today's beach is short, protected by two large outcroppings of rock so the water is calm and clear in a shallow bay. We sit in the water with our legs outstretched and let the cool water soothe our swollen bug bites.

There are only a few other parties on the beach with us and

it's a pleasant change from the previous days of crowds. Their conversations are soft, like whispers on the breeze and I only catch snippets as I start to doze off in the shade of a palm tree. *What should we do tomorrow? I can't believe it's our last day. I'll never stay at this hotel again. She said something about a flu going around on The Big Island. Do you think it will rain later? What if there's sharks in the water?*

I jolt awake with a shock, slapping my calf at an imaginary shark but it's only the wind that has blown my towel across my legs. I find Darren, stretched out beside me, staring at me fondly.

"Hey beautiful."

I smile, "How long was I asleep for?"

"Only 15 minutes or so."

"I feel so much more tired than before," I flop back down onto the blanket.

"Do you want to head back?"

I look at my phone and it says 5:58pm. "No, let's stay a little longer and wait for the sunset."

"Ok."

We enjoy the last moments of warmth beneath the cotton candy sky as day fades into night. We have another couple take our picture when the sun sits right on the horizon and the sky is streaked with pinks and reds and purples.

I feel a slight chill as the first star winks in the inky sky and Darren wraps his arms around me and rubs his hands up and down my arms to warm me. He kisses my hair at the temple and whispers, "I love you, Anna. I can't wait to marry you."

I lean deeper into him and smile. "I can't wait to have your babies," I say.

He chuckles as he says, "someday," and kisses me again before grabbing my hand and leading us back to the car. I'm silent for the short ride back to the house as his words sink in, leaving me feeling like I've just been punched in the gut. Someday? I step out of the car, my vision blurred for a second as anxiety surges through my body. What did he mean by that? I look down to the ring on my finger and tell myself it was surely a joke - Darren knows what I want, that I'm thirty-two and my time is running out. He wouldn't have proposed without being ready for it a family...right?

8

MARCH 2023

Anna

It's been three days since the *someday* incident – we've been ATV-ing and waterfall rappelling and snorkelling but every time I start to enjoy myself, Darren's *'someday'* ping-pongs back and forth in my mind and I return to a state of barely contained panic. We only have two days of vacation left and I can't go home without some clarity. I can't step back into our old life wondering if Darren and I still have different timelines.

"Dare…" We lie in our bed, naked with the cool sheets against our skin. He's propped up against the headboard reading through reviews of nearby restaurants, trying to find somewhere for dinner. I'm snuggled under his arm, lazily twirling his chest hair in my fingers.

"Mmm."

"What did you mean the other day. When you said someday."

"Huh?"

"When you said I can't wait to marry you and I said I can't wait to have your babies. And then you laughed and said someday."

"I don't think I laughed."

"Ok, chuckled, or whatever," I roll my eyes but he can't see because I won't look up at him. "So, what did you mean?"

"Just what I said. We will have kids someday. But let's get married first." He kisses the top of my head and asks, "how do you feel about sushi tonight? There's this roadside stand that's supposed to be amazing."

"But I was hoping to get pregnant right after the wedding," I don't mention that even before the wedding would be more ideal.

"Can't we have some time to ourselves first?"

"Time to ourselves?! We've had five years!" I exclaim shrilly. I try to calm myself down and the next statement comes out as a creaky whisper, "I've been waiting long enough."

"Well I can't give you an exact date, Anna. We'll just do it when it feels right."

"*Now* feels right! At least for me. It's felt right for years! You promised that we could have kids right after we got married."

"I never promised that."

"So, what would you call it then? What you said during our big fight on Halloween? Or do you even remember that fight?"

"Pretty hard to forget."

"So?" I ask, anxiety is growing in my stomach like a tumour.

"So…it was more like a suggestion."

"A suggestion?" I think I might vomit. Or have diarrhea. Or both. "We almost broke up. I only stayed because I took your suggestion for a promise."

That night, we climbed out of the Uber in front of our house, the air wet with the evening's rain, yellow oak leaves sticking to the bottom of our boots.

"Why does my sister think you're pregnant?" Darren asked me, looking down at a text on his phone

"Huh?" I ask tiredly, twisting the key in our front door, pushing it open and stumbling in, a little more drunk than I thought I was.

"Alicia, she thinks you're pregnant. She texted me."

"What did she say?"

"Congrats, winky-face, pregnant-woman emoji, don't worry I won't tell mom and dad."

"Oh."

"Oh?"

"Well, her friend Trina was pressuring me to do shots and when I declined she said, what are you, pregnant? I said no."

"So then why does Alicia think you are?"

"I might have winked...when I said it."

"Why would you do that?" He sounded annoyed, angry even.

"She was flirting with you ALL night! She does it every time we see her."

"Whatever, she was flirting with everyone. It's just her personality."

"Yeah, her personality is a leech. She wants anyone else's boyfriend."

"She's annoying but she's harmless. You don't have to go around spreading lies about being pregnant."

"Spreading lies?"

"Well it's not true is it?"

"No...But what if it was? Would it really be that bad?"

"Yeah."

"Why?"

"We don't want one right now."

"Don't say *we* don't want one. *I* want one!"

"What do you want me to say Anna?"

"That you're ready!" When he didn't answer me I demanded to know, "what are you waiting for anyway? You know that women have a biological clock, right? That my time is running out? My eggs are dying! Literally dying!"

"Don't be so dramatic, Anna."

"I'm not being dramatic. At the age of thirty a women has lost 90% of her eggs."

"That doesn't even sound real."

"GOOGLE IT THEN!"

"If all you want is a baby then go get one – you don't need me!"

"I don't want just *any* baby – I want YOUR baby!"

"I don't now what to tell you Anna. And I don't know why you have to keep bringing this up."

"Oh, what? Now I'm not even allowed to discuss my feelings with you?"

"I guess you just don't give a shit about my feelings."

"Your feelings?! You're getting exactly what you want!"

"Can't you see how much it hurts me though? I'm just trying to be honest with you and it fucking crushes you. You think that feels good for me? You think I want to do that?"

His outburst silenced me. I *hadn't* thought of how it must hurt him. Guilt cut through me but it didn't dull my own hurt.

"Sometimes I think it would be easier if we ended this. That it might be easier to lose you than to let you down again."

"No." I crossed the distance between us and wrapped my arms around him. He buried his face in my neck, surely getting blue body paint from my Avatar costume all over his face.

"I know you want me to be ready for a baby and that you

want me to be ready for marriage. It's a lot of pressure. Can we just focus on the marriage part first? We can have a baby after we get married."

I wanted to say ok and nothing more but I pushed him for reassurance, the anxiety in my heart demanding it. "When do you think that'll be?" I asked quietly.

"I don't know Anna," he said, his voice thick with frustration and his tears left trails in my body paint like scars.

DARREN

I'll never forget Halloween 2022, how she looked in her Avatar costume, how the blue face paint ran with her tears as I broke her apart.

Yeah, I remember talking about having a baby after I figured out the marriage part but I never expected Anna to demand it the minute I slipped the ring onto her finger. I still need time.

"What's so wrong with waiting?" I demand.

"I've already been waiting! I've spent five years waiting. What if I keep waiting and by the time you're ready, I can't have kids anymore?"

"That's not going to happen."

"You don't know that! It could have happened already," she hiccups with a cry before steeling her resolve, "I'll resent you Darren. If you take motherhood away from me, I'll always resent you."

"So I should just ignore my own feelings?"

"I'm not saying that but it feels like you're ignoring mine. I just don't get it. Why wait? We're getting married, you say you want kids, what reason could you possibly have to put it off? Especially if it means this much to me?"

"Anna, I don't know how else to explain it. I want to feel ready and right now, I don't."

Anna

There's really nothing more to say and the emotions are too overwhelming for both of us; the tears come and there is nothing we can do to stop them. Darren folds me into his arms and holds me, I feel his own tears fall into my hair but I can't bring myself to look up at him. We never make it out for sushi; we never make it out of bed. We spend the rest of the evening simply holding each other, slipping in and out of sleep, pulling each other tighter, closer, never wanting to let go but wondering if we have to.

9

MARCH 2023

Anna

We spend the last two days of our vacation in a daze. We are dulled, barely speaking, all we can do is hold on to each other, hands intertwined and clasping tightly wherever we go, bodies entwined every night, tears on our shoulders, in the crooks of our necks. I spend our last evening and the next morning in an intense state of panic. Can't eat, can't sleep, can't even breathe kind of panic. I'm not going home with Darren. I just don't know how to tell him that so I end up going with him to the airport, going through the motions of checking in and checking my bag. I sit with him as we wait for the boarding call, clasping his hand tightly, chewing the inside of my lip until I taste the iron of my own blood. Finally, the flight attendant calls for our row to board and here it is, the moment when I have to do it, the moment from where there is no going back.

"I'm not going with you."

"What?" Darren asks as he fiddles with the zipper on his backpack.

"I'm not going home."

"What are you talking about?" He turns to look up at me, confused.

"I'm not boarding the plane."

"That's…what? We have to go home; you have work on Monday. You checked your bag."

"I'll figure it out. I have to figure a lot of things out."

"What are you talking about?"

"I can't just go home and be your fiancé and act like nothing is wrong when we don't know if we want the same things in life."

"We do want the same things."

"Just not at the same time. Well, timing matters Dare. I've pictured my life a certain way and the years just continue to slip by with nothing changing. If we go home, if we just step back into our regular life, how are we going to figure anything out? Timing has been a problem for us for years – and we never figured it out. We need to do something different."

"Sure, I get that, but I don't think we should split up. We should figure this out together. That's what partners do, what married couples do."

"But we're not married," I say in frustration. "That's part of the problem; I wanted to be married years ago. And now, I…I don't know if we should." I chew my lip and twist my ring but I won't take it off. I won't give it back. Nothing has been decided yet.

"You can't be serious. What the fuck? All you wanted was to get married!"

"No, all I wanted…all I *want* is to have a say. You're not ready, I don't want to force you into anything, but just saying *no* doesn't give me any say in the matter. Don't you see that? You're just *telling* me to wait indefinitely. It's never been a fair discussion. And then you tell me I could just leave you, as if that's a fair alternative?"

"Is that what you're doing now? Leaving me?"

"No, I...I don't know. We just need some time apart."

"How much time?"

I just shrug in response. I can't answer that just the same as he can't tell me his timing.

"Let's not do this here. Come home and we'll figure it out."

"No. I meant it when I said we need to do something different. If I come home, we're going to fall back into our old routine and more time will pass and nothing will change."

"That's not fair, Anna."

"Yeah, well, it hasn't felt fair for awhile."

The flight attendant comes on the loudspeaker and announces the final boarding call and I can see the finality of what is happening reflected in Darren's eyes.

"Why did you even stay with me then?" He asks quietly, picking up his carry on and preparing to walk away.

"Because I've never met anyone like you and I've loved you in a way I thought was only meant for books and movies. I want to keep getting to know you as we navigate the next fifty years together, I want to keep loving you. I want you in every possible way...just not more than I want a family."

Darren doesn't say anything. I stare into his eyes and see a storm reflected back at me, dark grey like thunderclouds with a starburst of gold behind his pupil. They hold tears like a cloud holds raindrops. "I don't want to leave you," he says.

"I want you to." He gives me an intense stare before turning on his heel and boarding the plane without looking back.

As I find my way out of the airport, desperately trying to hold back my tears, my phone lights up with a text from Darren.

D: Where will you stay?

A: At Lisa's – they had a cancellation for one of the rooms in the main house

D: So you planned this.

A: I'm sorry. I don't know what else to do.

D: I hate this

A: me too

D: What about work?

A: I'll call Melissa. I'm sure she will let me work remote for a bit.

Three dots appear but no message follows. I imagine he's typing *what about me*, if I had a chance to respond I would have said *you'll be ok* but nothing else follows and I see his plane start to taxi away from the tarmac.

I make it out of the airport, stepping from the cool air conditioning into cloying heat and I almost breakdown. But I can't – not yet. With shaky hands, I order an Uber on my phone and ask him to take me to the nearest mall.

I purchase a sparse wardrobe, basic toiletries and the cheapest laptop I can find. Checking my bag was a mistake but I was cowardly, waiting until the last minute. If I hadn't though, he would have convinced me to come home, I'm sure of it. And I can't – I can't step back into our old life as if everything is ok because it's not. I deserve a say in the timeline of our life and I've taken a backseat for too long. So why do I feel like I've just made the biggest mistake of my life?

10

MARCH 2023

Anna

I'm not sure what time it is when I hear a gentle knock on my door. I'm lying in bed, eyes puffy from crying and hair matted from neglect. Lisa peeks her head in.

"Hun, are you doing ok? Do you need anything?"

"Mmm," I mumble groggily, waking from a terrible dream. "I'm ok. Just napping." Lisa walks into the room and gently closes the door. I can feel the sink of the mattress as she sits on the corner.

"Is it a nap if you never get out of bed in the first place?" She asks gently. "You've been sleeping for three days now. I'm worried. I know what you're going through – I was married once."

My eyes fill with tears. I don't want her to relate to my pain, I want to drown in it, believing I could be the only person who has ever suffered this way.

Lisa lays a light hand on my calf, "you're not going to figure anything out in here, life is outside this room and you need to try and live it. To see what you really want; to see if you can live it without him, or not."

"I know. But..."

"But you can't get out of bed?"

"Yeah."

"I can help."

"Please."

And with a nod she rips the covers right off the end of the bed and walks out of the room with them. It feels like she might have turned up the air conditioning before she came in here because I'm positively freezing. And I stink. Three days in bed without a shower was another bad idea of mine. I can't quite get out yet but I pull myself to a seated position and lean against the headboard. I wonder how I'm suppose to get on with living after kind-of-but-not-really-breaking-up-with-my-fiancé. I bet Amazon sells a handbook.

At home, I had a habit of running whenever I needed to escape my thoughts. The thought of punishing my body with exercise gives me hope that maybe my mind will shut up for a little while so I shuffle out of the bedroom and ask Lisa if she has any workout gear that I can borrow. She makes me eat a small breakfast of plain toast and fruit before she gives me a well-worn pair of Lululemon leggings and one size too small runners. I'm convinced there's no way I'll fit into the leggings because Lisa is definitely slimmer than me but it turns out that three days in bed wondering if you've just ruined your entire life was the diet I needed.

I see myself in the mirror and notice a gauntness in my face and a slimness in my thighs that I haven't seen in nearly a decade. I sit on the edge of the bed to tie the frayed laces of Lisa's running shoes and I debate getting back into bed, shoes and all. But I ignore the feeling and walk to the front door. I stand there for a moment, wondering where I can go that won't remind me of Darren but there's nowhere. I queue up my playlist on my phone and pop in my headphones.

I decide to go to the beach, even if memories of Darren will haunt me, because I like the way the sand is heavy, trying to hold me back. The runners pinch at my toes and my calves burn, requiring extra effort to balance on the uneven sand with each footfall. It's a punishing run and exactly what I need.

11

MARCH 2023

Anna

Lisa has been the perfect companion for my life falling apart. If not for her, I never would have gotten out of bed and she still makes sure I do each morning. She always has encouragement when I need it but at the same time, recognizes when I need to be alone. She feeds me because I can't manage to do it myself and hugs me whenever she sees the tears dripping down my face.

I've been "working" remotely for my company back in Canada but mostly I just stare at my computer screen dwelling on the choices I've made recently. I'm wondering when they're going to notice I'm not doing much of anything. My boss has been great really, she hasn't pushed me for details about why I need to be remote indefinitely and she's not applying her usual pressure to improve deadlines. So when I feel the need to go back into bed and cry, I abandon my computer and do just that.

Darren and I have texted sporadically in the days that we

have been apart but he hasn't responded to my last message (a GIF of a cat completely failing to make a jump) and I wonder what it means (does he no longer love me? is he totally over me? or is he more of a dog person than a cat person and he's mislead me all these years?).

I talk (ok cry) to Nat on the phone most afternoons (it's dinnertime for her in Toronto so I'm not sure how much she is *actually listening*. I mostly talk over her yelling at her son to not put food in his hair and at Chad to do something about it, she's *ON THE PHONE*.)

I will miss my call with Nat today though because Lisa has arranged for me to go horse-back riding. I must have told her at some point that I rode horses as a young girl and that I always dreamed of riding on the beach. She's surprised me with a private trail ride (I guess she knows I'm in no shape to be around happy tourists) and when I find out she isn't coming I beg her to join me but apparently she's terrified of horses.

My guide, Leilani, is a native Hawaiian who grew up on Maui and earned a university degree in Geology. She lost her job as a geologist during the 2008 recession and so she moved to Kauai and started the ranch. At forty her body is toned and lean, her face weathered by sun and salt and sand. She is bubbling with excitement and facts about the geology of the island as we set off on our journey and at first her enthusiasm makes me feel nauseous but as the horse's gait lulls me, I start to enjoy myself.

The ranch itself lays amongst lush rolling hills so we ride across open fields before we reach the coastal Maha'ulepu Heritage Trail. Eventually the tall green grasses give way to orange-brown earth and black, craggy rock. I ask Leilani why the volcanic rocks have so many craters in them and she explains that these craters are called vesicles, the cavities formed when a bubble of gas, trapped inside the lava, expands and then escapes into the atmosphere.

As we continue further down the trail, I have a hard time believing any of the landscape around me is real. To say the scenery is breathtaking is not enough, it's more like I will never breathe again. We follow the path up and down rugged cliffs, feel the spray of the waves as they crash against the stone walls and shoot upwards to shower us. Leilani points out the native flowers that grow, even in the volcanic soil. She shows me the nesting area of Ua'u kani sea birds and the sacred religious sites along the trail. We pass an isolated cove that has a black volcanic rock beach. The water here is darker and more turbulent than the clear turquoise waves washing against the white sand stretch we come upon shortly after. We see it from above first, the empty stretch before us, and then we ride down through the dunes to reach it. According to Leilani, this beach is the perfect spot to watch for pods of whales in the winter and sometimes you will see the endangered monk seals sunning themselves on the sand. I turn around in my saddle with a smile on my face, expecting to find Darren behind me and I'm blindsided by sadness when I remember I'm alone.

Settling back down into the worn leather, I try not to let his absence (or the reminder that it's my fault he isn't here) steal all my joy from the ride. Leilani and I dismount and walk our horses down the beach. She points out a family of sea turtles swimming away from shore and some bright, colourful fish swimming through shallow reefs. The beach is mostly deserted although there are a few wind surfers and kite-boarders in the water. At the end of the beach we tie the horses up and Leilani leads me to a small cave where we find sea creatures in the tide pools. I take off my boots and socks and slip my toes into the silky sand.

As I wander the beach, the sky becomes streaked with pink and orange and purple as the sun continues to dip below the horizon. I am reluctant to leave but eventually we remount and head back the way we came. The thought of returning back to Lisa's, to cry myself to sleep for another night, to wake up alone for another morning, makes me feel wild. So, the moment my horse steps off the narrow trail and into the rolling green field, I encourage her into a canter and then push her into a full out gallop. I pass Leilani and I let the wind whip the tears from my eyes.

12

MARCH 2023

DARREN

I've been home for almost a week and I can feel the distance between Anna and I like a taunt rubber band about to snap. I'm simultaneously angry with her and missing her and terrified of losing her. Part of me wants to call her and tell her to come home, that we'll have a baby right now but then I get angry again. Why is her *timeline* more important to her than me? If we're going to spend a lifetime together, what's another year or two of waiting? I know she's worried about her age but she's only thirty-two; we have lots of time.

I'm sitting on our couch wishing for the weight of her legs on my lap, even missing her annoying habit of burrowing her toes into my thigh when they're cold. I'm confused when there's a knock on the front door, no idea who would be visiting me. For a moment I think maybe it's Anna but when I open the door I find Nat standing in front of me.

Unexpected and unannounced, I have no idea why Anna's best friend is showing up here. She must know that Anna isn't here. I realize that Nat probably knew before I did that Anna wasn't coming home and I feel a twinge of anger again. Nat's probably furious with me for letting her stay, for not just knocking her up and giving her what she wanted. Nat isn't afraid to speak her mind, ever, so I'm expecting to get a full-on lecture but instead she crosses the threshold without a word and pulls me into a tight embrace.

I cough around the tears in my throat, surprised by the wave of emotion that her affection awakens. I feel my eyes water but a coughing fit gives me an excuse to pull away and explain away my inability to speak and my watering eyes. "Why is she doing this?"

Nat laughs, "she's about as stubborn as you are Darren."

"Fuck, what a pair we are."

"Tell me about it!" She walks past me and flops down on the living room couch. "Just to be clear, I'm loyal to Anna and always will be."

"I know."

"But I think it's completely irrational of her not to come home."

"Would you do me a favour and tell her that?"

"Ha! No way."

"Worth a shot."

"You two are so good together, I hope you figure this out."

We are good together – great together. I'm tempted to open up to Nat and tell her that I'm afraid to lose Anna to motherhood. She wants this so badly; does she even want me? I want to ask Nat if she knows what *ready* is supposed to feel like. I've been waiting for it, even trying to will it but I don't know, sometimes

I still feel like a kid myself.

Nat must read my confused expression as she softly explains, "I know that Anna wants you to want this. She wants you to feel good about becoming a dad. She doesn't want you to do anything you don't want to." Anna always claims that Nat is a mind-reader and I finally get it. "Anyway, do you want to watch The Bachelorette with me?" she asks, already reaching for the remote.

"Not really," I laugh, feeling the tension leave my body.

"Well too bad, because it's Tuesday and I always watch The Bachelorette at your house on Tuesdays."

"With Anna."

"Yeah, well, you'll do," so I sit with her and watch it, thankful not to be alone.

13

MARCH 2023

Anna

It's hard to believe that two weeks have passed since Darren got on that plane and I didn't. I don't think that staying behind has given me any clarity because I still want Darren, with my whole heart, I still want him but I still want to have a baby. *Now* – before my eggs die and my ovaries close up shop.

I wish I would have been more prepared for how hard love actually is. The bullshit romance novels and movies (which I love to read and watch) give girls and women this impression of sincere, romantic, idealistic futures that life doesn't live up to. You're putting two people into one life – how is that ever easy? But the story is always about how they found each other – not how they manage to put up with one another for 10, 20 or 50 years.

I remember being fourteen and desperately wanting a boyfriend. Shane was my crush at the time and I would live on

MSN Messenger whenever I wasn't in school, waiting for him to sign on in the hopes that he would chat with me. When he did sign on but didn't start a conversation I would toggle my status from appear offline to online about a million times so that he would get the little ~*~Anna <3~*~ has signed in notification. If that didn't work then I'd put his favourite song on repeat so my status would read ~*~Anna <3~*~ is listening to Life Is A Highway and that never failed (which is stupid because it was always the same song, like I must have been so obvious).

I used to daydream about losing my v-card on the pool table in his basement. Not exactly romantic and definitely not practical but it would have been better than the anti-climatic three minutes I had on a basement couch a few years later.

I laugh at the memories of my naïve, fourteen-year-old self and pull out my phone to text Nat.

A: Remember Shane?

N: Your high-school pool table fantasy?

There's really something amazing about having such long-term friendships.

A: Yeah

N: Didn't he pick you up at the mall?

A: MSN me sometime. Oh yeah

N: lol oh the MSN days

A: Ever miss them?

N: fuck yes.

N: remember how we would send each other every message for approval before sending to a boy?

A: LOL, I feel like I should never have stopped. Maybe I wouldn't be in Hawaii alone

N: I def would have told you it was a bad idea

N: But you wouldn't have listened anyway. You never did back then either, you always said what you wanted to say.

A: So I've always been an idiot 🏚️

N: 😀

N: did you see the bachelorette last night? 🌹

A: no, there's no cable here. Do I want to know what happened?

N: Antonio punched Derek! In the face!

A: What?! No!

N: a cameraman broke it up!

A: ok that's crazy. I'm going to have to Youtube this shit.

N: I watched it at your place

A: you did?

N: yeah. last week too

N: Darren thinks Mark should win

A: WHAT?!?! a) NO Mark is a dick b)Darren watched THE BACHELORETTE? c) did you have to give him a lobotomy first?

N: a) agreed - huge dick (but prob has a little dick)

N: b & c) maybe he just likes me better than you

A: a) micro penis fo sho

A: b &c) I can't blame him, you're kind of the best

N: when are you coming home? He's a wreck.

I type and erase and type and erase.

N: I'm not saying you have to be with him, but you should figure this out together.

I have no idea what to say so I put the phone down and in the morning I will tell her that I fell asleep even though I know she'll know that's bullshit.

14

MARCH 2023

Anna

The next morning, I wake slowly, the bright sunshine coming through the thin curtains and stinging my eyes. I reach for my phone but then pull my hand away. I don't want to find a text from Nat calling me out and I don't want to find out that Darren *hasn't* texted me. I asked him yesterday how his day was going and he read it but didn't reply. I bite the bullet and grab my phone to find that it's the opposite – no message from Nat but one from Darren; *Bad. They're all bad. I miss you.* The tears start flowing immediately. I rest my phone facedown on my chest, sink lower into the pillows and cry.

I'm full of mixed emotions and I need to clear my head before I text him back so I go for a run which has become a ritual for me over the past few weeks. Each day I become more accustomed to the heat and the heavy sand and I can run a least a kilometer farther than when I first started. Today I push myself ever further and approximately half an hour later I'm staggering on weak legs, ready to collapse. I've run down the beach until reaching the end where it leads into cool, shaded jungle. It's as good a place as any to give up. I fall gently into a seated position on the sand, crossing my legs. I pull my phone out of my pocket and pausing my music, I bring up his message and reread it at least five times. I miss him too but do I tell him that? Does it change anything?

I'm breathing heavy – from the run, from the hope, from the fear of what any of this means. I text him back, *I miss you too. I'm coming home.* With a fearful squeal, I throw my phone away from me and lie back in the sand. I look up at the sky trying not to think about what I've just set in motion and what he might say in response. I will my breathing to come back to normal and when it does I finally sit back up. Taking in my surroundings, I realize how secluded this part of the beach is. No one is around but me.

Without thinking too much about it, I remove everything except my underwear and wade into the cool ocean waves. They wash the sweat and fear from my body. I dip my head under the water, running my hands through my tangled hair. I don't want to be apart from Darren any longer; I'm ready to figure this out together.

After my swim I take a few moments to myself, laying out in the warm sand and letting the Hawaiian sun dry the water from my skin. The dried salt leaves faint, wavy lines across my bare stomach. When I hear voices approaching from down the beach I dress quickly and walk back to Lisa's.

My thoughts are consumed with second-guessing my decision to go home but in the end, it feels right and I determine everything else is just fear. My stomach pulls my attention as it growls with hunger, catching me by surprise. My appetite has all but disappeared lately and I've barely eaten a full meal since Darren left. What I have eaten has been hard to keep down because my anxiety over everything has been making me so nauseous.

As I reach the house my phone dings with a notification from Uber Eats as if it's reading my mind. I swipe it away, thinking that I've spent too much money on take out already – I'll cook for myself today. But then the thought of my own cooking makes the nausea come back and the hunger disappear. It's safe to say that I'm not the most gifted in the kitchen. Darren isn't great either but he's better than me. No wonder I'm such a fan of take out. And so bad at dieting.

But I need to eat and I'm determined not to have take out again so I plan to bike into town and grab something simple to cook. When I reach the house and round the corner to grab my bike, I notice a surfboard leaning against the yellow siding that wasn't there before. I'm wondering who it belongs to when I turn around and bump right into the owner.

"Shit, I'm so sorry!" I say, my face pressed to a man's bare chest. It's a very well muscled chest I notice. I step back quickly and look up at him, "really sorry," I say again, taking another step back when my foot catches on my bike's kickstand and I lose my balance, falling to the ground. The bike and surfboard both tumble down after me, landing on top of me.

I push myself up on my forearms, my head poking up through the detritus of my clumsiness and my cheeks burn with embarrassment as the man I ran into laughs gently. I can feel my face wearing a scowl but I guess it is pretty funny. I laugh awkwardly as he deftly lifts the bike and board off of me. He offers a hand to pull me up and when I take it I notice a small tattoo on the inside of his wrist, the outline of a wave. When I'm standing again I find that I have to tilt my neck back to look up at him. He's tall. Like, tall, tall. I'm not short or anything (*Nat is short*) but my face only reaches his chest. He's also tanned; really tanned; his skin golden against the stark contrast of his navy-blue swim trunks. They hang low on his hips, abs cutting to a seductive V that makes my pulse race.

Hurriedly, I redirect my gaze to his face and find bright blue eyes flecked with green and lined with dark lashes. His mop of dirty blonde curls hangs over his forehand and he has a large, boyish grin that reveals a single crooked tooth. It's charming and I can't help but smile back at him.

"Hey, I'm Jack," he says, still holding my hand.

"Anna." I pump his hand once and when he withdraws it he shyly swipes his curls off of his forehead.

"Nice to meet you," he says. My skin is hot all over.

"Likewise. Is this yours?" I ask, pointing to the surfboard.

"Yeah, I just checked in this morning. Here for a surfing trip."

"Fun," I say for lack of anything else. Clearly, I don't know how to talk to good-looking men in person – on a dating app *maybe* but even then…oh god, the thought of making a Tinder profile today is terrifying. It was hard enough when I was still in my twenties. If Darren and I don't work out and I have to join the dating scene again, I'm doomed.

"So, where are you off to?"

"Town. I need groceries," I say lamely. I'm truly doomed.

"Mind if I join you?"

"Uh, sure. Just let me get changed quickly." He nods and when I jog past him to the front door I notice that he smells of sunshine (how is that even possible?).

A few minutes and change of outfit later, I find Jack sitting on the front steps waiting for me, a second bike at the bottom of the stairs next to mine.

"Ready?" He asks. I nod in reply.

Thankfully Jack is very chatty and I avoid embarrassing myself further. He talks as we bike leisurely into town. By the time we reach the grocery store and lean our bikes against the side wall, I've learned that he's originally from Vancouver but lives in Whistler; he's 29 and the second-oldest of 4 brothers; this is his fifth time visiting Hawaii and third time on Kauai. In the winter he works as a ski instructor on Whistler's Blackcomb mountain and in the summer he's a line cook at a busy restaurant in town. He asks me about myself, where I'm from and how long I've been here and I answer without mentioning Darren.

As we stroll through the small grocery store Jack asks me what I'm cooking tonight. I can't bring myself to say Kraft Dinner (the only thing I've thought of that I'm confident I can't screw up) so I just shrug and say "I'm not sure yet". He asks me what my favourite foods are and I rattle off a long list. Just because I can't cook doesn't mean I don't love to eat.

It isn't until we near the checkout that I realize my basket is essentially empty while his is full of the ingredients to make my number one favourite, spaghetti carbonara.

"Oh my gosh, I haven't really been paying attention have I? I should run back and grab something I can actually eat," I say, looking down at the stick of deodorant and box of Q-tips in my basket (*what do I need these for?*).

"Why don't I cook tonight?"

"Oh – you want to cook for me?"

"Yeah, why not? Cooking for one is never fun."

"Mmhmm."

"So it's settled?"

"Sure. But let me buy the groceries. And we should invite Lisa too." I don't want him to think this is a date; it's definitely not a date.

"Sounds good to me."

It's already mid-afternoon by the time we make it back to the house with our groceries. Jack says he's going to head to the beach and catch a few more waves before dinner so I retreat to my room and start looking up flights home. There are a couple of options with long layovers and a direct flight later in the week. I go back to my text messages with Darren and check that my last one *I miss you too. I'm coming home* was delivered. It was. I stare at the message and the blank space where he should have responded. I toss my phone across the bed, wondering why he hasn't written back yet, wondering if he doesn't want me to come home.

I wake to the smells of garlic frying in a hot pan. I turn my phone over and realize that I must've fallen asleep. Two hours have passed and the sky outside has darkened. Darren still hasn't responded to my message so I leave my phone in my room and make my way to the kitchen to find Jack at the stove. I ask him what I can do to help and he hands me a knife and a leafy green bundle of parsley, asking if I can dice it.

When he sees me chopping the herb into quarters he says, "uh, actually, if you could set the table, that would be great."

"No problem," I say enthusiastically, dropping the knife and moving over to the cupboard. I have no idea how to "dice". I grab plates from the cupboard and lay them out on the dining table with cutlery as Jack takes over the parsley, chopping it into fine slivers. Oh, well that doesn't look *too* hard.

It doesn't take long for the meal to be ready and soon Jack, Lisa and I are sitting around the table laughing over empty plates and a bottle of wine. The food was delicious and my stomach is settled for the first time in days.

Throughout the evening I notice that Jack spends more time talking to Lisa than he does to me and I feel guilty for ever thinking he might construe this as a date. He is clearly just a very friendly guy. They talk animatedly about the islands, the best surf spots and the best places to eat. I'm happy to sit quietly and listen to them banter back and forth. Jack has an easy laugh that he shares often.

Lisa launches into stories of past guests and we end up spending hours around the table. She's a natural storyteller and has met so many people from all over the world. It makes me think that I'd love to own a bed and breakfast one day.

Eventually she rises and clears the table, ordering us to stay put while she washes the dishes. Jack and I stay seated at her insistence and he directs the conversation towards me. I tell him about my work as a product manager for a software company back in Toronto and how I'd love to actually renovate my Victorian fixer-upper of a house but never find the time. When he asks me about my parents I start to tear up but I manage to tell him I lost my Mom during the COVID-19 pandemic without letting them spill over. I breeze past my Dad, just saying he was never in the picture before asking him to tell me more about his family.

Neither of us ask about our respective relationship status which I'm thankful for because what would I say? It's complicated? As if it's a 2009 Facebook status update?

When I can't stop yawning I decide it's time to call it a night. The bang of pots and pans in the kitchen sink quieted awhile ago and Lisa never reappeared so I can only assume she retreated to her own room. As I say goodnight to Jack, I ask him if I can buy him lunch tomorrow, to repay him for the amazing dinner. He says yes, but only if we go to his favourite roadside sushi stand. I wonder if it's the one that Darren found with the rave reviews. We never did make it. I agree to his terms and say goodnight, turning on my heel quickly before he sees the tears that thoughts of Darren have stirred up.

15

MARCH 2023

Anna

The next day I shuffle into the kitchen feeling exhausted even after ten hours of sleep. "Good morning," I say blearily to Lisa as I enjoy the soothing feeling of the cool tiles on my bare feet.

"Morning!" Lisa chimes back.

I grab a piece of pineapple from the large platter of fruit that is ever present in the kitchen and pop it into my mouth.

"How did you sleep?"

"Mmm, not great," I say around a melon ball. "I should let you know that I'm going to be going home. I found a direct flight and I fly out in three days from now."

"Oh, I'll miss you but that's great. Does that mean you've worked things out with Darren then?"

"Not really. I still want Darren and I still want a baby. But I realize now that we need to figure this out together. I don't regret taking some space but it's time for me to go home now."

For a moment my thoughts dwell on it *not* working out and I'm filled with an instant panic that steals my breath and sends a jittery adrenaline rush through my veins. My chest heaves as I try to pull in enough oxygen. I don't want Lisa to notice my panic so I try to distract both of us by asking, "did the other guests arrive last night? I didn't hear anyone."

"No, they cancelled too. I guess the whole family is sick. That's the third booking now, all due to the flu. Or so they say."

"That's last minute. Do you have to refund them?"

"I don't have to but I will. It doesn't feel right to keep their money when they can't stay."

"Sure, but it's not like you even have an opportunity to rebook the room."

"It's fine. My mortgage is already paid off. I just do this for the company," Lisa says with a smile.

"Your guests *are* pretty cool," I say and she laughs. I turn my attention back to the fruit platter and select a piece of mango. Before I can eat it the overpowering scent of it hits my nostrils and makes them flare in disgust. But I love mango. Has it gone off? I inhale deeply again and the scent makes me gag. Fuck. I'm definitely about to vomit. I look for the garbage can to throw out the mango but it's not there – Lisa must have taken it out for garbage day. I'm not sure what to do when I gag again so I just stuff it in my pocket and run for the bathroom where I proceed to puke my guts out.

Lisa knocks on the door a minute later asking if I'm ok and I tell her to come in. I roll from my knees to my bottom, sitting with my back against the bathtub. Lisa hands me a glass of water and I take a long pull.

"You ok?" Lisa repeats her question and my answer is to

throw up again.

"Oh hun, what did you eat last night?"

"Roadside sushi. Ugh, I knew it was too good to be true."

"From Mariana's?"

"Uh huh." I nod weakly.

"Huh, can't be food poisoning then. She has the best sushi in all the islands."

"But I didn't eat anything else," I take another sip of water hoping to keep this one down.

"Morning!" I hear Jack shout from the kitchen.

"Morning Jack!" Lisa peeks her head around the bathroom door, "how are you feeling today?"

"Great!"

Lisa nods and closes the door. She takes a seat on the edge of the bathtub and rubs small circles on my back. t makes me think of my mom and how, whenever I was sick, she'd spend the day watching movies with me and let me drirk Gingerale and she'd rub my back until I fell asleep. The memory brings a knot of tears to the back of my throat.

"When was your last period?" Lisa asks, bring ng me back to the present.

I wave the thought off, "It's definitely the roadside sushi."

"But Jack is fine."

"Then it's probably stress," I start to say even as I start counting back the weeks in my head. When was my last period? When was the last time I took a pill? I'm reminded of that nagging feeling I had the first night in Hawaii; that I forgotten something. I realize now that it was my birth control pills, lost under the couch with my favourite lipsticks. "Maybe we should get me a test," I whisper to Lisa before I puke once more.

She rubs my back some more before telling me to stay put, that'll she'll pick up the test for me. She leaves me with a cold washcloth on my forehead and a refilled glass of water. I sit with my back to the bathtub and my head tipped backwards, eyes closed. My throat burns like I've been drinking cheap whisky.

When Lisa returns and hands me a pink cardboard box, I just sit there staring at it for at least ten minutes. This isn't my first pregnancy test and I already know what to do but I pull out the instructions anyway, just to stall for time. I have no idea what I want it to say.

I've taken a few tests throughout the course of my relationship with Darren. Once when we first started dating and I definitely wasn't ready. My period was a day late but the test was negative. And then a few years later, when I was ready but he wasn't, I'd get my hopes up that my pills had failed us. Anytime my boobs were super sensitive or my period lighter than usual, I would take a test, convincing myself there was a chance. But the tests were never positive.

Today, there is a chance. I haven't taken a pill since the day I arrived in Hawaii and it's safe to say that Darren and I had *a lot* of sex during our 10 days here. I pee, cap the test and throw it into the sink where I can't see it. I set a timer on my phone for three minutes

Today I don't hope for anything because I don't know what result I want to see. I don't want it to be negative but I'm not sure I want it to be positive either. It wasn't supposed to happen this way. I should be at home, in my ensuite bathroom with Darren outside the door. I should be excited, happy, sitting here with my fingers crossed.

When the timer goes off, I don't even want to look but I

know I have to. I grab the test from the sink but before I can even glance at it I have to puke again. I'm sitting on the closed toilet seat so I lean over, holding the shower curtain out of the way, and vomit into the bathtub. I already know what the test is going to say. Pregnant.

I clean up the tub and rinse my mouth with mouthwash. I come out to find Lisa puttering around the kitchen, picking things up and putting them down in the same place. Just trying to keep her hands busy while she waits for me.

"I'm pregnant," I say and she envelopes me in a huge hug without a single word. She's rubbing my back and I close my eyes as the tears start to fall. I've never wanted my mother more than in this moment and the absence of her makes this so much harder but I still find comfort with Lisa. Her embrace is completely neutral, no congratulations, no apologies. She lets me figure out my feelings on my own. "I don't know what I'm going to do," I whisper.

"You'll figure it out," she says with a pat, pulling back from the embrace. "I'm here for you, whatever you need."

"Thank you. I think I just need to be alone right now."

"Ok hun."

I decide to go for a walk to clear my head and I start towards the beach in a daze. When I arrive I fall cross-legged into the sand and watch the waves lap the land in a rhythmic motion. I hug my knees to my chest and let my chin rest on them. I let the tears silently slip behind my sunglasses as the sun's shadow moves over me like a sundial.

I have what I've wanted for so long. The thing I've secretly hoped would accidentally happen with each passing month has *actually happened*. But will Darren believe me that it was accidental? Will he hate me? Is there still going to be a chance for us? And what will it look like? Will this always sit between us?

I am overshadowed by guilt. I've made him a father when he isn't ready to be one and I have no idea how he's going to respond. What if he doesn't want to have anything to do with the baby?

I pull out my phone and bring up our text conversation. His response two days ago to my message that I was coming home was so encouraging then.

D: thank god. when? I'll pick you up

D: I love you

But now? Now everything has changed. I start to sob, rereading the messages only brings me more heartache. What if he doesn't love me after this? What if I have my baby but I don't have him? I've realized too late that he means more to me than having a family.

13:26

Saturday, April 1

NEWS   30m ago

BREAKING NEWS

Epidemiologists have identified a new strain of the
Coronavirus originating from the United States. More
details to follow.

NEWS   16m ago

POLITICIANS AND CELEBRITIES SPREAD MISINFORMATION

Misinformation and false claims about the new COVID
variant are already being widely shared online. Read our
fact check report with real-time updates as more details
emerge.

NEWS   4m ago

CANADIAN PRIME MINISTER TO ADDRESS THE NATION

The Canadian PM will hold a press conference later today
to address the reports of a new strain of COVID and what
this means for Canadians.

16

APRIL 2023

Anna

The minute I see the news notifications on my phone I'm reminded of my mom, dying alone in a crowded hospital, of the nurse trying to hide his tears as he held a tablet above her prone form while I said goodbye. That was 2020, that was COVID-19 and now? A hard pit of fear materializes low in my belly and my breath comes in shallow gasps. I lay a hand on my stomach, protective of the baby inside me. Trying to keep the panic at bay, I call Darren.

"Dare, what's going on?" I ask before he can even say hello.

"I don't know. It seems like there's a new variant of COVID."

"But they said it was over. We had Omicron and everyone got it and they said it was over," my voice rises with my panic.

"They're calling it COVID-23."

I start to cry, "what if you get sick? What if Nat gets sick?" *What if I get sick and lose the baby?* My cries turn to sobs, "I can't lose someone else, Darren, I can't."

"Hey, it's going to be ok."

"What if I can't come home? What if they lock us down and I'm stuck here?"

"That's not going to happen."

"You don't know that! God, what have I done?" I cry into the phone.

DARREN

"You're going to come home Anna, don't worry."

"You don't know that," she cries.

She's right, I don't know that, not with complete certainty anyway. The news networks are constantly tweeting breaking news and it feels like everything is changing by the minute. Still.

"Look at the evidence. During the first pandemic, we never closed our borders to Canadians. All you needed was a negative test and you could get on a flight home. So that's all it's going to be, if anything. Your flight is tomorrow, nothing is going to happen before then."

"Are you sure?"

"I'm sure." I'm not.

"Shouldn't I get on a flight tonight?"

Should she? No, there was no other direct flight and at this point she can't get across the border before tomorrow and there's no point in ending up somewhere in the middle of nowhere, America. No, she's safe where she is. "Nope, just try to get some sleep tonight. It'll be a long flight tomorrow."

"Darren, I…" she hesitates and never finishes her thought.

"I love you, Anna."

"I love you too."

My own anxiety was low level when I ended the call with Anna a few hours ago but by the end of the workday everyone has stopped working and they huddle around each other's desks talking about COVID-23. I hear someone say that Reddit is blowing up with reports of flights being cancelled and European countries closing their borders. I take a look for myself, hoping it's just anti-vaxxers and trolls spreading rumours but I'm worried all the same.

I leave the office half an hour early, unable to sit at my desk with all of this nervous energy. I feel the urge to run to my car but I make myself walk at a normal pace. When I get there, I don't know where to go so I text Nat and while I wait for her to respond, I try calling Air Canada to confirm Anna's flight. I keep trying despite continuously getting a busy signal and when I'm finally connected to the automated menu it says there is a 13 hour wait.

"FUCK!" I slam my fist against the steering wheel. What the fuck do I do now? Just then my phone dings with a reply from Nat. She's home. I put the keys in the ignition and head towards her place. At every red light my hands grip the steering wheel so tight the leather creaks. The traffic is heavy and it takes me half an hour to reach Nat's when it should only take ten. When I knock she shouts for me to come in and I find her in the kitchen wearing an apron, flour handprints decorating the black fabric, kneading a loaf of bread.

"What are you doing?"

"Making a sourdough. Lockdown seems inevitable, don't you think? I'll probably be laid off again and Chad will have to close the bar. We'll be broke, or, like, more broke. The least I can do is enjoy gaining my COVID weight." Her voice is shaky with nerves.

"But what about Anna?" I ask sharply. I get that Nat's afraid, that this will affect her life too, but I'm pissed that she's making bread when she should be trying to help her best friend.

"What do you mean? Anna is flying home."

"Tomorrow."

"Yeah…" She doesn't get it.

"The border might not be open tomorrow."

"What?!" Nat shrieks. "That's a lie. It's not true."

"It's all over Reddit."

"What's Reddit?"

"How do you not know what Reddit is?" I bark through gritted teeth.

"You don't have to yell at me!"

"I'm not yelling!" I yell and she starts to cry. I feel instantly guilty. I shouldn't be mad at her, it's not her fault. "I'm sorry."

"Maybe COVID-23 isn't going to be that bad," Nat's voice is weak like she doesn't believe herself.

"Then why are you baking bread?"

She looks down at her bread, "I didn't mean to," she punches the loaf with an unexpected anger. A few tears fall leaving stains in the flour. She looks back up to me. "What are we going to do?"

"I was hoping you would tell me."

17

APRIL 2023

DARREN

I spend the night at Nat's trying to get through to any airline that flies in the US but with no luck. Now it's 7am and I'm watching the news anchor announce the closure of the US-Canada border. They don't have many details yet other than that it takes effect immediately. Anna won't be flying home.

My skin is tingly, like there's bugs crawling beneath it. My breathing is low and shallow; my heart is pumping furiously. It's probably a panic attack but I really don't have the fucking time.

It's the middle of the night in Hawaii right now and I'm thankful that Anna's asleep while this is happening. It buys me some time to figure something out before she wakes up.

"Nat!" I shout, hoping she can hear me in the other room. She left to change Logan's diaper just before the announcement. "They're doing it – they're closing the borders."

"What? I can't hear you!"

"Come here for a sec!"

"I can't, I've got too much shit on my hands!"

"What?!"

I said, "I've got too much shit on my hands," she says as she pokes her head around the corner a minute later. "It was an explosive diaper." Nat walks back into the living room and Logan crawls in after her, gurgling happily.

"You're not great at selling the idea of parenthood," I quip.

"It's not gross when it's your baby."

"Uh-huh, I'll take your word for it."

"So what did you want to tell me?"

I suck in a deep breath wishing we could just keep joking about baby shit but we don't have much time. "They're closing the borders," I say and I watch the news sink in until her body folds in half. "Incoming travellers can't come in. They're turning planes around."

"No," she says simply as she collapses to a seated position on the floor and starts to cry. "I can't believe this." Logan crawls into her lap and her tears fall onto his head of soft baby hair. "What are we going to do?"

"Do you still have those local government phone numbers from last lockdown when Chad was petitioning the restaurant measures?"

"Yeah…but they're complete tits. It never helped, we almost lost the bar and they didn't care."

"It's better than nothing." I feel dejected at her negativity.

"I know, I know. What about outgoing travellers?"

"What do you mean?"

"Can we leave the country? Go to her?"

I never even thought of that. How did I not think of that?

I'll beat myself up over it later. I shoot up from the couch and grab my sneakers. "It's worth a shot."

I stop at my house on my way out of the city to grab my passport and I forget to lock the front door behind me but I'm not turning around now. The traffic on the highway is the worst I've ever seen it and today I am that douchebag that everyone hates - the one that swerves from lane to lane, taking any open spot. When I finally arrive at the airport, I drive straight to departures and abandon my car in the no parking zone.

There's a crowd around the doors and everyone seems upset, shouting and pushing. I elbow my way to the front of the crowd and yank on the closed doors, straining my shoulder when there's no give. The doors are locked. "What the fuck is going on?" I ask the crowd at large but no one seems to hear me. I run back to my car and drive like a madman to another terminal.

There I find a set of open doors and as I slip through, I notice a group of security guards walking towards them. I head in the opposite direction, jogging to the first airline desk I see. There's a woman already at the desk arguing with the stewardess and I wait impatiently behind her, shifting my weight from foot to foot.

"But I have a ticket!" the woman shrieks as she waves a piece of paper in the stewardess' face.

"Ma'am, I'm very sorry but this is completely out of my control."

"There must be something you can do."

"I'm so sorry, but all planes are grounded."

"I'm an American citizen," she slams her passport onto the desk. "You have no right, NO RIGHT, to tell me that I can't go back to MY COUNTRY."

"I understand how hard this must be."

"NO. YOU DON'T. How could you possibly understand?" I can see the stewardess' compassion turning to anger. "Do you have a husband and two kids back in Texas, huh?"

"Ma'am–"

"Don't you ma'am me. I don't care what you say. I know my rights and you can't keep me out of my own country."

"You know what, *Karen*, you aren't the only person who's stranded. I do have a husband and kids and they're in Atlanta and I'm here so don't act like you're the only one."

The woman gasps and her entitlement reaches an whole new level and her voice a whole new octave. "Did you just call me Karen?! Oh, you are going to pay for this. I'm going to have you fired!"

"Get out before I call security," the stewardess says with a sigh of exhaustion.

"EXCUSE ME?!"

"I said, GET OUT BEFORE I CALL SECURITY." The woman is shocked enough that she shuffles a few feet away, tugging her suitcase behind her like it's the one who has offended her. She pulls out a phone and turns back to glare at the stewardess as she dials. When her call connects she turns away and says "speak to a supervisor," to what must be an automated menu.

"Good luck with that," I hear the stewardess whisper under her breath as I step forward.

She doesn't acknowledge me so after an awkward moment of silence, I speak first, "I need to get on a plane to the US. Anywhere but preferably Hawaii. My fiancé, she's alone." She looks at me blankly for a minute before breaking out into tears and without a word she walks away from the desk and through an *Employees Only* door.

I feel a hand on my shoulder and turn around to find a man standing behind me. "I'm trying to catch a flight too but they're saying no one in or out. We're all stuck here."

Before his words can really sink there is a message over the loudspeaker. *'Pearson Airport is now closed. All arrivals and departures are cancelled. Everyone other than ground crew must leave the airport. Please follow all instructions from the security guards and allow them to direct you to an alternative exit.'*

At that moment, a group of security guards approach us and herd us away from the airline desks. As we shuffle down the hall, I notice the doors that I entered through are now locked and a crowd has formed on the other side, just like at Terminal 3. They're banging on the doors, begging to be let in. We keep walking until we reach gate 3D where we take a jetway to the tarmac and from there are lead to the front of the terminal. I make my way back to where I abandoned my car and thankfully find that it's still there – I guess they don't care about parking violations when the world is ending – and I climb in and drive away in a daze.

When I call Nat and tell her what happened she takes over, speaking with her usual authority. This is the Nat I need, the commanding paralegal that takes control of the situation and makes shit happen. She tells me that we're going to call every "asshole" in the government that agreed to this closure and we're going to bring Anna home. We have a couple of hours before Anna wakes up in Hawaii and discovers the news and we can't waste a minute of it.

PRIME MINISTER ANNOUNCES CLOSURE OF CANADIAN BORDER EFFECTIVE IMMEDIATELY

In an unprecedented move, the Canadian Prime Minister has announced that the Canadian government will be closing the border to all incoming travelers, including Canadian citizens and permanent residents. Flights that are currently en route have been advised to turn around as their landing authority has been revoked. The Prime Minister had a message for citizens who are currently abroad.

"To my fellow Canadians, do not think that your government is abandoning you. We are not. We will do whatever it takes to beat this virus on home soil and we will work tirelessly to bring you home once the global situation has stabilized and it is safe to do so. Know that I do not make this decision lightly and I trust in our allies to keep you safe while you are away from home."

Phone lines to all of the major airlines have been tied up since the news broke as Canadians

18

APRIL 2023

Anna

When I wake the next morning and see a message from Darren saying *call me* 🌑 I know something is wrong. I swipe his message away and bring up my news app to learn about the border closure. I rush to the bathroom and promptly throw up.

I desperately want to hear Darren tell me it's going to be ok (even if I won't believe him) but I reminded of the secret I'm keeping from him and it feels impossible to talk to him right now. So, I call Nat instead.

I'm crying before she can even pick up the phone and she keeps saying "it's going to be ok" while she waits for me to catch my breath.

"I guess you saw the news?" She asks. Why does she sound so calm?

"Why didn't I come home? Why didn't I just get on that damn plane?"

"You thought you were doing the right thing."

"But what if I never make it home?"

"Never? Come on. This isn't The Hunger Games," she quips but it just makes me cry harder.

"I'm not strong enough for this."

"Anna, you're the strongest person I know."

"But I'm alone."

"You're not alone! You have me and Darren. We're ontop of this. We'll figure something out and get you home. In the mean time I'll send you so many cat GIFs you'll want to block my number."

"Promise?" I ask through my tears – cat GIFs *are* the best remedy for any problem. Nat's response is to send me a GIF right away and I laugh. "I still wish I had come home with Darren."

"Like I said, you thought you were doing the right thing. And it's not like you could have predicted this would happen."

Not the border closure, not the pregnancy. "Nat, I'm..." but the words won't come out of my mouth no matter how badly I want to tell her. Darren deserves to know first.

"You're what?"

"I'm scared."

"We made it through the last pandemic. We'll make it through this one too."

"But what if Darren doesn't want me when I come home?" *What if he doesn't want this baby?*

"Well, that's the dumbest thing you've said in awhile."

"I've probably ruined everything," I start to sob, thinking about our baby and wondering if he'll believe me that it was an accident.

"He loves you," Nat says quietly. "I know that now more

than ever. Seeing him these last few weeks, I've never been more sure of you two. But hey, worst case scenario, you break up and then you go back to dating and you'll probably meet Zac Efron or at least a decent look-a-like and you'll have incredibly hot sex and you'll be pregnant with beautiful babies and by then Darren will be nothing but a distant memory."

I laugh involuntarily and there is an unflattering snot bubble involved; this is the Nat I know, erasing my anxiety with her humor. "As if online dating in your thirties is that lucrative," I say.

"It can't be all bad."

"Think of all the unsolicited dick pics I'd get."

"Like I said, not all bad!"

19

APRIL 2023

Anna

At the same time the border closure was announced, the state of Hawaii enacted full lockdown measures. That was less than two weeks ago and everyone has slipped back into lockdown mode as if we never left it. The current C23 restrictions are all too familiar – non-essential businesses are closed, social distancing is required and masks are recommended. Considering that much of Hawaii's commerce is tourism, many jobs have been lost yet the people of Hawaii are meeting this second pandemic with Aloha - kindness, compassion and faith that everything is going to be ok.

Ontario is, of course, locked down too so Nat and Darren are both working remotely for now. Nat is convinced that she will be laid off in no time. I was laid off immediately. Thankfully I was still able to apply for the government of Canada's COVID unemployment benefit online and I'll receive the first of my monthly deposits tomorrow. This will allow me to still cover the bills at home and pay Lisa who is letting Jack and I stay here indefinitely. She doesn't want much – certainly not her usual nightly rate – just some help with groceries and utilities. Lucky for all of us that her mortgage was paid off years ago.

As much as I wish to be home, I am grateful to be going through this with Lisa and Jack. I couldn't imagine being alone in 200 square foot room within a tall glass hotel like so many other tourists. The three of us mostly do our own things during the day but during the evenings we binge-watch British crime dramas (Lisa's favourite) over bowls of microwave popcorn.

During the day I try to escape reality through reading but I'm finding it harder and harder to concentrate now that I'm rereading one of my vacation books for the third time. It's during a fading afternoon that Jack finds me on the front porch hammock staring at the pages of my book. He's back from surfing, his curls barely dry and dripping water as he climbs the wooden stairs of the porch. He has his surfboard under his arm and the sun behind him is an orange ball as dusk descends. He surfs every day and sometimes I'll walk down to the beach and watch him from afar. You wouldn't think he's scared or anxious about this pandemic at all if you saw him on the waves but when the three of us congregate around the dining table each night, you can tell how much he misses his family.

"What are you reading?"

"It's called Second Best."

"Any good?"

"It is but I've already read it twice so I'm not that into it. I only brought two books with me on vacation and now that the stores are closed, I can't get anymore. Lisa only has true crime novels and they freak me out," I shiver.

"What about e-books?"

"And burn my retinas by reading on my phone all day? No thank you."

Jack laughs at my dramatic answer as he turns toward the surfboard rack on the other side of the porch. I take in his long and toned torso, drops of water glittering against his skin. His feet and calves are speckled with sand from the walk home. I watch the muscles in his arms and shoulders grow taunt as he lifts the surfboard and places it on the rack. "Shrimp tonight?"

"Sure, let me just finish this page and then I'll be in to help."

"That's alright, enjoy your book."

"Come on, I can't be that hopeless," I say with a laugh. Jack has been trying to teach me how to cook but I think it's been harder than he expected.

"Uhhhh–" he says, drawing it out with a smile so I know he is at least half joking. "Alright, give me ten minutes though? I'm going to jump in the shower first." I nod in reply and he heads into the house. A second later the porch light turns on above me and my page is illuminated in the fading twilight.

20

APRIL 2023

Anna

When I wake up a few days later, I shuffle out of my bedroom, rubbing the sleep from my eyes and I almost trip over something right outside my door. It's a pile of worn paperback books. I bend down to pick them up and see a yellow sticky note on top of the first cover. *I don't know if these are any good but it was all I could find - Jack.*

My heart swells a little, overcome by Jack's kindness. I sit cross-legged on my bed and read the back covers of each book, eager to choose my first read. All are well-read with dog eared pages and cracked spines. There are two bodice-ripping romances, a horror from Stephen King and a pocketbook on Hawaiian plants. There's another note on this last one, *maybe we try to find some of these?*

Jack knocks on my half-open bedroom door as I'm in the middle of reading the synopsis of the romance novel and I involuntarily blush as I look up at him.

"Morning."

"Morning! Thank you so much for these books. Where did you find them?"

"Passed by a garage sale and picked them up. I hope you like them." When he says garage sale I can hear my mother's voice in my head asking *what about bed bugs* but I brush the thought away because I'm desperate for something new to read.

"I love them."

"Good, guess what else I found at the garage sale."

"What?"

"You have to guess."

"Ugh, I have no idea, I didn't even think garage sales were still a thing," I laugh.

"Just one guess."

"Ok, vintage Playboys?"

"That's your guess?"

"I don't know!" I whine as we both laugh.

"A Nintendo 64."

"What?! No way! That's SO much better than old Playboys."

"Well, I don't know about that…" Jack teases.

"I'm really secretly hoping that it came with Mario Kart because I used to *slay* at Mario Kart back in the day."

"Oh really? Because it just so happens that it did come with Mario Kart."

"Think your ego can handle losing to a girl?"

"It doesn't need to, I never lose."

"Challenge accepted," I laugh, abandoning my new books on my bed and following Jack to the living room, ready to beat his ass.

We spend a good portion of the morning playing Mario Kart and I find out just how competitive Jack can be. We're evenly matched at this game and when either of us loses we demand another round to redeem ourselves.

We laugh and taunt each other as we crash our cars together on the screen and throw insults across the couch.

21

MAY 2023

Anna

It's been a month since the border closed and I've almost come to accept this as an extended vacation. Nat and Darren talk to me every single day and keep me positive. They keep me believing that this is temporary but this morning I wake up to the last messages I will receive from them without knowing they are the last ones. I lay in bed, quickly write back to Darren that I did and it was delicious and then send Nat a long line of lol's. I put my phone down and fall back into the pillows without realizing that neither message says *Delivered* beneath it.

I think of another boring day stretching ahead of me and wonder what I'll do. Should I start my next book or help Lisa categorize her pantry? Or ask Jack for another cooking lesson? In the last month we've learned that COVID-23 – or C23 as it's now called – is more contagious than the original strains of COVID-19 and the death rates are higher. As a result, Canada's lockdown measures are coming from the federal level and none of the provinces have looser restrictions like they did last time. Even America is trying to do the same. The President has issued executive orders to mandate lockdowns but some states (not Hawaii) are fighting back. Anti-lockdown protests have turned to riots in many cities and have resulted in deaths over the past few weeks. More police officers have died in the line of duty in the last month than in all of last year.

I would be more scared if I didn't feel far removed from it. Things are calm here in Hawaii. Similar to COVID-19, warmer countries aren't subject to such high transmissibility because of the outdoor lifestyle. On top of that, everyone is acting respectfully, wearing their masks indoors and honouring social distancing. Even the tourists – we're all just grateful to be taken in and cared for by the locals.

My phone makes a weird chime, pulling me from my thoughts. It's a notification to tell me that my texts didn't go through. I try sending them again and decide to get out of bed and find some breakfast. I pull on some track pants and head out to the living room where I find Lisa standing in front of the TV watching the news with a look of shock on her face.

"We have confirmed reports from the White House that the President of the United States has activated the internet kill switch in response to the spread of misinformation online as well as the organization of violent protests. This includes mobile phone networks which will no longer operate. Just last week a record number of 43 police officers were killed in the line of duty across this country as the May 1st Freedom Protests took place. The President has this message for Americans: "The internet is a danger to the health and safety of Americans across this great

country and as the death toll from C23 continues to climb, we must focus on saving the lives of as many Americans as possible. We must stop hate and misinformation in its tracks. Now, more so than ever, we cannot be a divided nation."

The news anchor seems to be in shock herself as she reads the statement.

The last month has been so filled with anxiety and fear – of getting sick; of a loved one dying; of never coming home – but I never could have imagined this. I didn't even know an internet kill switch existed. Dumbly, I take out my phone and try to Google *internet kill switch America* but the screen just reads NO INTERNET with some suggestions on running diagnostics. I guess it's real. My phone chimes again with the notification that my text messages didn't deliver. I realize that I don't even get the chance to say goodbye.

I start to fall apart – slowly at first until I completely shatter. I hold Lisa's hand as we change channels only to find breaking newscasts interrupting every station. As if in a trance, I walk to the kitchen and grab a plate, layering it with pieces of fruit from the usual spread. I take one bite of a pineapple and then I throw it all in the garbage including the plate. I stand at the kitchen island with my hands balled into fists, slamming them against the granite countertops until I can feel bruises forming, blood beneath the skin. Jack materializes from nowhere and gently but firmly grabs a hold of my wrists and stops me from punishing my hands any further. I yank my arms from his grasp and turn towards him with anger and fear in my eyes and an argument on the tip of my tongue but before I can say anything he hugs me, whispering in my ear, "I'm in this too," and then I break.

I sag into him, letting him hold my weight, tears streaming

down my face and I can't stand anymore so I sink to the floor until I'm crouched with my knees clasped between my arms. Jack joins me on the floor, pulling me closer to him so that our knees touch and his strong arms can wrap around me. I sense Lisa behind me and feel her hand rubbing small circles on my back. I want to reach out a hand and offer her some comfort too but it's beyond me now. I drop my forehead to my knees and stare into the darkness of my own shadow and I cry, I sob, I scream. I let the world know that I recognize everything that has been taken from me.

22

MAY 2023

DARREN

It's been days since I lost contact with Anna but I keep texting her anyway. I guess it's a defense mechanism to pretend that this isn't happening; that I haven't lost her. Every message remains undelivered and unanswered.

D: I love you

D: I miss you

D: I'm going to find a way to fix this

D: How do you get Nat to stop talking? She's talking about a mucus plug and I want it to stop…

I swear, the news coming out of the US reads like something out of a conspiracy theory and I can only hope that Anna remains relatively untouched in Hawaii. There are reports of every other state in America struggling with protests and high death rates, but Hawaii is rarely mentioned.

Life here feels exactly like COVID-19 – schools are closed,

non-essential workers are working remotely, and toilet paper is hard to find. It feels so familiar that you almost wonder if the freedom of 2022 was a dream.

As a game developer it was easy for my job to be transferred to a remote position once again and I don't miss my office friends like I did the first time around. I'm alone and I just want to sink into that loneliness.

I'm hardly working and I wonder if and when my boss is going to notice but in the end I don't give a fuck. Let them fire me. I stare at lines of code all day but all I can think about is Anna and the future we might have lost. What is anything worth if I can't share it with her?

Any of the anger I felt towards her for abandoning me at the airport is long gone and instead I blame myself for leaving her there. I never should have gotten on that plane.

Nat is the only thing keeping me sane right now. She's the only person I see, I've even shut out my family. One of the Covid restrictions is to not visit other households and I just keep pushing off my parents by telling them we need to follow the rules. I want to protect them but more than that I don't want them to ask me about Anna. They know she didn't come home with me but they don't know why. They know she's stuck there and I can't handle them asking if there's been any responses from my calls to government officials. Because the answer is always the same – I've made no progress.

I want to protect Nat as well especially because she's high risk at five months pregnant, but she waves off any worries I have of transmitting the virus to her. She reminds me that I'm barely leaving the house even to feed myself so she's not concerned. We break the rules every week when she sneaks in through my side door with a grocery bag full of junk food to watch the latest episode of The Bachelorette. Honestly, I think she ends up rewatching it when she gets home because she mostly talks throughout the whole episode. She tells me stories of Anna in high school that I've never heard. Nat also keeps me distracted with her own stories - office drama among the paralegals, an affair between two of the lawyers and anecdotes about pregnancy that I never wanted to hear.

23

JUNE 2023

Anna

Has it been days since I've spoken to Darren? Or weeks? I don't even know anymore. What's the point of keeping track of time when I've lost everything? There's a little voice in my brain asking, *what about the baby,* but I ignore it. I feel disconnected from everything, the baby most of all. Sometimes I wonder if it's even real or if it was all a dream.

I have no energy to do anything but I know I need to get out of bed. I don't go far. Most days I drag my duvet off the bed to the living room and lie on the couch watching the news. The TV still works and rumour has it so do landlines but who has one of those anymore? America has become unrecognizable, just like my life.

Protests and riots continue – did they really think people couldn't organize a protest without social media? Hospitals are so overwhelmed that they're turning people away, leaving them to die at home. It's very reminiscent of Italy at the beginning of COVID-19. To make matters worse, doctors and nurses are quitting by the hundreds as they can't cope with a second pandemic. Especially when sick patients still claim that the virus is a hoax.

Lisa hovers over me like a concerned mother hen and I hear her cluck to Jack, "she shouldn't be watching this, I think it's making her depression worse."

I'm not depressed, I want to say but I just shut my eyes, hoping to shut out her worry and everything else too.

24

JUNE 2023

Anna

A week later, in a hushed whisper, I admit to Lisa that I'm not sure if the baby is even real anymore. She encourages me take another pregnancy test right away and when I see the positive result I hug myself and cry and cry and cry.

When all my tears are spent, I look up to Lisa through wet lashes and whisper, "I need some help."

"Ok honey," she says, smiling at me kindly. "Let's go get some." Before I can let the desire to climb back into bed change my mind, we're in the car driving to the walk-in clinic.

It's a short drive to get there but a long line to check in. It snakes outside the front door and around the corner. I'm about to suggest we turn around and go home when Lisa hands me a KN95 mask and says, "it'll move quickly." I put it on as well as a second cotton mask and we join the line.

It does *not* move quickly and I want nothing more than to go home but I think of the baby growing inside me and I feel a spark of joy which gives me the resilience I need to wait. I lay a hand over my belly. I can feel that it's grown already. You can't tell to look at me but I can feel it in the hard, swollenness – as if I just ate a whole pizza to myself. I decide that it's going to be a girl.

When we finally reach the reception desk I take in the tired nurse behind the scratched plastic barrier. You can tell she's exhausted by the dark bags under her eyes and the smeared mascara. I wonder when she last had a good night's sleep. She pulls down her mask to take a sip of coffee and the mask has left marks on her face that are so deep and red they look like scars.

Lisa knows her – it's a small island after all, everyone knows everyone – and there's a moment of small talk before Lisa explains that I'm pregnant and we suspect perinatal depression and we'd like to see a doctor.

The nurse's eyes are full of regret when she says, "it's a sixteen hour wait and most everyone here is sick with C23. I think it's best if you just go home."

I can tell that Lisa is distraught, but I squeeze her arm and say, "it's ok, let's just go."

"Is there *anything* we can do?" Lisa asks the nurse.

"I heard that Jerry might have come out of retirement. Maybe you can set up a counselling session? He's still on Coconut Lane."

"Thank you, Mikala. Hang in there."

Lisa drives straight to Coconut Lane and I stare out of the window watching the palm trees sway in the stiff ocean breeze.

"I don't think I can talk about this stuff with a man," I say as we turn into a gravel drive. The lane is lined with palm trees and I can see a glimpse of the ocean on my left. At the end of the lane there's a large house painted a vibrant yellow with a pink front door. A patterned hammock sways between two trees on the front lawn.

"I know it's harder than talking to a woman but trust me, Jerry is great. I've worked with him, everyone has. He's been the only counsellor on this island for over 30 years and he finally retired in 2019. No one came to replace him."

"That's bad timing," I say, thinking of how the first pandemic started in 2020.

Lisa and I climb the steps of the large wrap-around porch. The house feels inviting with pots of flowers on either side of the front door. When we knock we're greeted by a woman in her late thirties who turns out to be Jerry's daughter and impromptu receptionist. She confirms that Jerry is taking patients and that he has an opening in forty minutes if we're willing to wait. Lisa and I head back to the car where we roll the windows down and push the seats back, settling in for the next forty minutes.

"Can I ask why you went to see Jerry?"

She takes a moment to respond before turning to me and confiding, "I lost a baby."

"Oh. Oh Lisa, I'm so sorry. We don't have to talk about it."

"It's ok. It was a long time ago, *obviously*," she teases.

"Not *that* obvious, aren't you only like forty-eight-ish?

Lisa laughs, "thank you darling but no, more *fifty*-eight-ish."

"What happened," I ask tentatively.

"There were complications," she says simply as her eyes start to fill with tears. "Her name was Kaila."

Silent tears slip down my cheeks as I reach across the center console and squeeze Lisa's hand.

"My marriage didn't survive it. He had his own way of dealing with the loss and I had mine. We couldn't help each other so in the end we parted ways. And I found Jerry, he helped me."

I think of Darren and how he cared for me when my Mom became sick and eventually passed away. I feel so much gratitude for him in this moment and I wish he was here now. I know he would take care of me and the baby.

I start to tell Lisa about my Mom and the panic attacks and the depression after her death. I tell her how she was such a vibrant, strong woman who raised me all on her own. She was so excited for grandkids but counselled me not to put too much pressure on Darren, that it would be worth the wait. *I wouldn't change anything about my life,* she once told me, *but being a single mother is the hardest fucking thing you can do.* As I share this with Lisa I realize for the first time, at least consciously, that I will be a single mother. Stuck here in Hawaii, I will be alone.

I'm pulled from the realization when Jerry's daughter approaches the car and tells me I can come in now. Lisa says she is going to go pick up some groceries and will be back for me in an hour.

When I meet Jerry, I feel instantly comforted. Even though half his face is covered by a mask, I can tell from the way his eyes crinkle that he is kind and gentle with a wide smile. He's likely in his seventies with tanned and wrinkled skin from years in the sun and salt breeze. His voice is deep and warm and he feels like a loving grandfather. I sink into a well-worn leather armchair and I immediately open up.

An hour later I climb back into Lisa's car and reach across the console to hug her with tears in my eyes. "Thank you," I tell her. "Thank you."

25

JUNE 2023

Anna

One of Jerry's suggestions – along with weekly visits – is to practice daily yoga to help ease the depression. He even got down on the floor and showed me some specific postures. "Normally I would just recommend a Youtube video," he said, looking at me from between his legs in happy baby pose, "but can't do that anymore." He is surprisingly flexible for his age.

Lisa joins me in my yoga practice every morning and I'm grateful for her companionship. Some days are harder than others but there has been a loosening somewhere within me.

Most days we take towels down to the beach and spend half an hour in various yoga postures before running into the waves and cooling off. Jack follows us with his surfboard and rides the waves while we're contorting our bodies. I find my eyes are drawn to him often, preferring to watch the way his muscles move beneath his skin than pay attention to Lisa and the next posture in the sequence. I'm always losing my balance.

Jack and I have picked up the cooking lessons again and each evening is spent in the kitchen. We talk about everything – our lives, politics, past accomplishments and hopes for the future – as we chop and dice and sauté. Sometimes it feels like a date and sometimes that feels good.

I think about Darren less and less now. I find it too painful. Jerry asks me not to avoid the pain but try to accept it. Sometimes I can and sometimes I can't. Either way, Darren is not apart of this life. He is apart of some other life, some other storyline. Jerry agrees with me that I need to focus on the good things that are here, in front of me. Jack is a good thing.

I can feel something building between us, it's reflected in his eyes when I catch him looking at me. I never mention Darren to him and certainly not the baby either. It would be too weird to bring up now after all this time. I'm barely showing but my body is changing. Does he notice? Does he wonder why I only wear a one-piece bathing suit now or why I never have a glass of wine with dinner?

PART TWO

Summer

2023

26

JULY 2023

Anna

July brings with it sticky, cloying heat and C23. On a Wednesday morning, I wake up with a sore throat and a wheezing cough. A rapid test confirms C23 and I cry knowing that I have to spend ten days isolating alone in my bedroom. The first few days are spent in bed plagued with fatigue and chills and aches. My throat is raw from all the coughing and I worry about the baby constantly. Will C23 have any affect on her (I had an ultrasound last week that confirmed it's a girl)? How bad will it get and will we be ok? I worry about where I picked up the virus and whom I may have given it to but Lisa and Jack are fine. Lisa drives to Jerry's to make sure he is ok and his daughter informs her that Jerry is as healthy as a horse.

Lisa and Jack lay meals and medicine outside my door for me but I barely eat because of how much it hurts to swallow. On the fourth day Jack brings me a tub of ice cream with a note,

Maybe this will go down easier?

Sometimes Jack will sit on the other side of the door and regale me with stories about his baby brother who is an aspiring stunt double. Jack thinks he belongs on the set of Jackass more than he belongs on the set of an action movie. I love hearing about his family – a household of 4 boys and parents who are still very much in love. I tell him that I hope I get to meet them one day and when he responds with *they'd love you* I get the sense of a deeper meaning.

After ten days of isolating I finally leave my bedroom. Lisa basically force-feeds me a huge breakfast of bacon and eggs and fruit and then pushes me to get into my bathing suit and follow her to the beach for yoga. We need to get back into the habit she tells me. I do as I'm told even though I still feel groggy with fatigue. I know she's right and besides, I'm excited to see the ocean and feel the sun on my skin and the sand between my toes. Jack comes along with his surfboard of course.

Lisa and I set out our towels on the sand and begin with a few cat/cows. I try to move through a flow practice with her but I end up just sitting and staring at the ocean. Before long, Jack comes running over and offers me a hand.

"Come, on, I'm going to teach you to surf. Have you ever surfed before?"

I think back to the surfing lesson I had months ago when I was just *on vacation*. I'm reminded of how the instructor taught me on the beach first, touching my legs and back to teach me the correct posture. I think of Jack doing the same. "No, never," I say, slipping my hand into Jack's, I let him pull me to my feet.

Jack lays his board in the sand near the water's edge and demonstrates what I need to do before letting me try. I lie on the board and then pop up into a crouch and Jack gently corrects my position. My skin is hot everywhere he touches me. His hands begin to linger as he moves my legs into the proper position and his thumb strokes soft circles at the small of my back.

"Maybe you'll do better in the water," he says distractedly. We wade into the shallows but the cool ocean does nothing to temper the heat between us.

The deeper we wade, I see Jack's expression turn to focus and concentration. With his hands on my hips, he helps me to get onto the board so I'm straddling it. He pushes the board over the lip of the waves, waiting for the perfect one. All I can think of is his solid body behind me and his strong hand splayed at the small of my back. I feel a heat starting between my legs and rushing up my body until it steals the breath from my throat. I turn to face him, intent on tasting him but suddenly he's saying, "ok, here we go," and he's turned the board to face the beach. I'm caught off guard and almost fall right off the board as he spins it forward but somehow I find my balance again and when the wave comes, I know what to do and suddenly I'm standing and riding the wave until the water meets the sand.

With a whoop of excitement, I jump off the board and I punch the air above my head. I can't believe how alive I feel and all I want is to do it again. My desire is completely forgotten, replaced with this powerful thrill. Picking up the board, I run back into the water, back to Jack who is laughing with me. We spend hours in the water and I feel more like myself than I have in months.

27

JULY 2023

Anna

After so many sub-par dinners, I can't believe that Jack still lets me in the kitchen. He is determined that I will learn to cook. I think he finds my ineptitude in the kitchen hilarious and I must admit that I enjoy his teasing.

There have been a couple of times when he has left me alone for only a few minutes to return to a disastrous mess of spices and sauce. I swear they jump out of the jar of their own accord when I'm not looking. And of course he was shocked when I admitted that I can't tell one herb from another. The next night he brought home every herb the grocery store had. He crushed them between thumb and forefinger, releasing the fragrant scent and waved them under my nose one by one. I was too distracted by the smell of *him* – sunshine, sand and ocean – to notice any of the herbs.

I would like to think that I'm not completely hopeless though.

He has taught me how to properly hold the blade of a sharp knife and I'm no longer afraid to pull the largest from the chopping block. Every so often he comes up behind me and curls his left hand over mine, reminding me to protect my knuckles from the knife's blade. "Can't beat me at Mario Kart if you lose a finger."

Tonight we have the kitchen to ourselves. When we come home from a long day of hiking, we find a note from Lisa on the kitchen island telling us that she's at a friend's place for the night and will be back in the morning. It's still against the restrictions to visit different households but I understand just how important it is to be with friends during times like these. It's worth the risk.

"Let's do something easy tonight," Jack says, clearly tired from our hike. We took the pocketbook of Hawaiian plants that he bought me at the garage sale and went searching for some of the more rare flowers.

Jack opens the cupboard doors looking for inspiration. He finds a jar of Tikka Masala and pulls a package of chicken breasts from the fridge. "This'll do. Want to get some rice started?"

"You know what, why don't you take a seat and have a beer," I say as I take the chicken from him. "I think I can handle this."

"You sure?"

"Yeah."

"Ok," he draws it out so it sounds like he doesn't believe me but he's smiling. Grabbing a beer from the fridge he sits down at the kitchen island and I can feel his eyes on me as I move around the stove.

It's less than ten minutes before Jack is up and taking over, guiding me with gentle instruction. I'm frustrated with my failure and I give up on the rice and decide that, at the very least, I can open a jar of sauce.

A minute later Jack catches me struggling and offers to help.

"Nope! I got it." I decline, flashing a false smile because I *don't* got it. I turn away from him and grab the dish towel and fold myself at the waist, using all my might to open this damn jar. How will I ever be a single mom if I can't open a fucking jar? Under my breath I mumble, "I'm a strong capable woman, I can open this jar."

"Huh?"

"Nothing," I say through gritted teeth.

"Chicken's ready," he says, turning off the burner, "why don't you let me help you," he reaches an arm around me to take the jar at the same time I turn towards him. At that moment, the lid finally gives. The sudden release of pressure shocks me and the jar goes flying from my hands. Sauce lands *everywhere*. Floors, counters – I can even feel it in my hair.

With a completely straight face, Jack picks up a strand of my sauce-coated hair, saying "not sure I like this colour on you."

"Har, har, har." I wipe my face and my hand comes away covered in orange sauce. Quickly, I rub my hand through Jack's hair. "Looks worse on you."

"Oh, you're going to regret that," he says as he reaches for me. I squeal and barely escape his grasp as I run around the kitchen island. I turn to face him, the large slab of marble between us and stick out my tongue playfully. He comes after me but I'm too quick – that is until I slip in the sauce covering the floor. Jack catches me but the momentum brings us both down to the floor, sauce everywhere.

Once the laughter subsides and we're able to get stable footing, we take one look at each other, sauced from head to toe, and we start laughing again.

"I think we need a shower."

"You're literally dripping," I say, grabbing the bottom of his t-shirt and before I can think anything of it, I lift it over his head.

"Yeah, we don't want to track this all over the house," his voice is husky, his laughter replaced with desire. He slips the straps of my dress over my shoulders.

"It would be rude to," I say, staring into his eyes as I pull on the drawstring of his shorts. I wonder what I'm doing but his lips look so inviting. He reaches around me for my zipper and he undoes it slowly as if he's asking for permission. I step closer and lay my hands on his bare chest, closing my eyes I focus on the feeling of his heartbeat beneath my palm. This connection is what I've been craving.

My eyes flutter open as I feel him lay a gentle kiss on the tip of my nose. His tongue darts out to taste a drop of Tikka Masala at the corner of my mouth and I know I can't take this slow burn anymore. I grab a fist full of curls and pull his mouth to meet mine. He tastes of coriander and ginger.

We make out like desperate teenagers and his desire is as apparent as my own. In the blink of an eye the rest of our clothes are gone and he's leading me down the hall to the bathroom, orange footprints in our wake.

We both step into the tub and he runs the water hot. Removing the hand-held shower head from its holder high on the wall, he brings it close to me, rinsing the sauce from my skin and hair. The water massages me and his mouth follows everywhere the water touches until I'm overwhelmed with desire. I take the shower head from him and rinse his hair and back while he folds himself around me, hands running down my back and cupping my ass, a nipple between his teeth and two fingers inside me. I can feel the tension building and as much as I'd love to extend this foreplay, I need more. I turn the water tap to cold and he shouts in surprise.

"Take me to bed," I say with smile. He growls and picks me up, stepping out of the tub and carrying me to my room. Along the way he lays kisses along my neck, my collarbone and my chest. We fall into bed, our wet hair dampening the pillows.

Hovering above me, his biceps flexed as he holds himself up, Jack stares deeply into my eyes.

"Please," I whisper desperately, and he slips into me without further hesitation. Our mouths are molded together as our bodies find a balanced rhythm. His left hand is in mine, our fingers intertwined, while his right lifts my hips so that he can thrust deeper inside me. He moves faster and faster and I arch my back in pleasure. He trails his tongue down the length of my neck, kissing the hollow in my collarbone. I bring his face back up to mine and kiss him, rocking faster and faster against him until we both climax, the sounds of our pleasure muffled by our kiss.

Spent and satisfied, Jack rolls off of me and pulls me into his arms. I lay my head against his shoulder and plant soft kisses on his chest. My eyelids are heavy with sleep and I'm struggling to keep them open. I feel safe in Jack's arms and I want to sink deeper into the feeling, into him.

"Jack, I…" *think I'm falling for you* I'm about to say but then the baby kicks and panic starts to rush through me.

"Hmmm?" He asks sleepily.

I sit up quickly and bring my knees to my chest. My skin is flushed and my heart is beating relentlessly. I grasp my hands together to keep them from shaking as I try to control my breathing.

I think about the baby, about Darren and how I've kept it all a secret from Jack. I *am* falling for Jack but I'm still in love with Darren. But will I ever see Darren again? Will we even have a chance at a life together? Would he even still want one? But why would Jack want a life with me either when I'm pregnant with someone else's baby? When I've lied to him for months?

Jack must sense a shift in the atmosphere because he blinks open his eyes and asks me what's wrong. I can't answer him, I can only shake my head as my breath comes in short, wheezing gasps. He sits up against the headboard and pulls me into his lap so my back rests against his chest.

"It's going to be ok Anna. Just try to match my breathing." He lays one hand on my chest and I stare at it as it rises and falls with my breath, at first fast and then slower and slower. When I've calmed down, I pick up his hand and trace the outline of the delicate tattoo on the inside of his wrist.

"Are you feeling better? What got you so upset?"

I take a deep breath, knowing I've got to tell him no matter how much I wish I didn't have to. "I'm pregnant," I stare at the bedroom door, waiting for him to walk out of it but he just chuckles softly.

He squeezes my bare shoulder and lays a kiss there, "I'm no doctor but I don't think it happens that quickly."

"No, you don't understand, I *am* pregnant."

"I should have had a condom, I'm sorry. I just got caught up in the moment.

"Jack, I – "

"If you're really worried I can grab you Plan B from the

pharmacy tomorrow."

"You're not listening."

"I can go now then?"

"No! You don't get it. I'm already five months."

"Pregnant? Five months pregnant?"

"Yes."

"Oh." When he doesn't say anything else I turn around to look at him. "So I guess it's not mine," Jack says awkwardly and I burst into tears. "Fuck, sorry, I didn't mean...I don't know what I meant but I'm sorry." He lays his hands on my upper arms and tries to pull me back to him but I'm already shuffling off the bed. I head to my dresser and pull on a pair of track shorts and a tank top and then turn back to the bed.

"No, it's fine. It's no one's baby but mine. I'll probably never see Darren again, anyway."

"I'm guessing Darren is the father?"

I nod in response. "We were engaged."

"Were?"

I shrug because I don't know how to explain it and my eyes fill with tears. Jack has tugged the bedsheet to his waist and I get the feeling he isn't comfortable around me now. "It's complicated. We were here on vacation and he proposed but we got into this big fight about our future. About kids. When it came time to go home, I couldn't go with him," I look down to my bare ring finger. My hands were swollen and I had to take the ring off. I thought it was water retention from the heat but then I found out I was pregnant. My fingers have become more and more sausage-like with each month. "Just before the border closed I decided I would go home, that we'd figure it out together. But then I was stranded and I found out about the baby. The baby he doesn't want."

"Is that what he said when you told him?"

"It's what I know. I never got the chance to tell him but I know. I finally heard him, I finally listened to what he's been saying all this time." A sob escapes me. "I'm all alone Jack."

"Hey, you're not alone," he slides off the bed, wrapping the sheet around himself and lays a hand on my shoulder. "You've got me and Lisa. We're your friends and we're not going anywhere." When he says the word *friends* I shrug off his hand and step away, his rejection stinging like a burn.

Before anything else can be said, the smoke alarm in the kitchen goes off. "Oh fuck, the rice!" Jack exclaims, dropping the bedsheet and bolting from the room butt naked. A minute later I hear his *fuck*s coming from the kitchen, the sound of a pot being thrown into the sink and then finally silence as the alarm is pulled from the ceiling.

When he reappears in my doorway he's holding a throw pillow over his junk. "It's a mess in there."

"I'll get started on the clean up while you get dressed."

"Thanks," he says and as I approach him I desperately want to kiss him. I want to go back in time to ten minutes ago when it felt like we were falling in love. The feeling was completely unexpected but if I'm being honest, it felt good; really fucking good. But friends don't kiss so I give him a fake smile as I pass through the door, taking care not to touch him.

28

AUGUST 2023

DARREN

"Do you still think about her?" Nat asks me out of the blue. We're on her couch watching an episode of 90 Day Fiancé. First The Bachelorette and now this but at least it distracts me from my real life.

"Of course. You and I talk about Anna all the time."

"I know, but like, what about when you're not with me? Do you think about her?"

"I can't stop."

It's August and I can't believe how much time has passed since I last talked to Anna. Even longer since we touched. We should be hanging out with friends at backyard barbeques and heading into Algonquin Provincial Park for camping trips. We should be planning our wedding. But without Anna, I don't want to do anything.

Now that COVID restrictions have loosened somewhat with

the warmer whether, my friends are going out, and carrying on with their lives. I watch it all through my Facebook feed and I turn down any invitations they extend to join them because I don't know how to explain Anna's absence or what that means for my future.

I've seen my parents a few times because there is only so much avoiding they will let me get away with. They worry about me and I wish they wouldn't. Nat is the only one I'm truly comfortable around these days. She's the only one who gets it.

Nat pauses 90 day Fiancé and turns to face me. "What do you think would have happened if she had come home? Would you guys have stayed together?"

I pause and take a moment to consider Nat's question. I know that I'm miserable without her but it doesn't really solve the whole *kids* issue. I haven't even given fatherhood any thought since the virus resurfaced. I guess I haven't really figured anything out. But I'm not exactly ready to admit that to Nat so instead I opt for humour and optimism. "Yeah, I probably would have knocked her up in the airport bathroom," I joke with a wide grin. Nat coughs on the candy she's eating, laughing.

"TMI, Darren! T.M.I."

"Yeah right. I've overheard your conversations with Anna for years. Nothing is TMI for you. I honestly think I know more about your sex life than I do my own," I say and Nat howls with laughter.

When Nat stops laughing and wipes the tears from her eyes she presses play on the show only to pause it again a minute later. "I think she'd want you to be happy."

"What do you mean?"

"She might never come home," Nat voices what I've been

fearing for some time now.

"She will," I say without any conviction.

"But she might not, and I know she'd want you to be happy."

"With someone else?"

"Yeah."

"How am I supposed to do that?" But Nat just shrugs, looking sad. "Do you think she's moving on?"

"I don't know. A small part of me – very small – hopes so? As much as I want you two to be together, I don't want to imagine her going through this alone. Does that make any sense?"

"Yeah." Nat's words hit me in a way I didn't expect – at first I was laser focused on bringing Anna home and after repeated failure, I focused on the absence of her and my own loneliness. I gave thought to how hard this must be for her, being cut off from me, her friends, her old life, but I never dwelled on it. Now when I allow myself to picture her all alone, it's tragic. But the thought of her finding comfort in another partner is heart-wrenching.

The thought plagues me for weeks and I can't get it out of my head. The mental image of her building a future, a life, a family with someone else haunts me.

29

AUGUST 2023

Anna

It's been almost a month since Jack and I hooked up and he has been true to his word – I haven't lost his friendship. Only thing is, I can't shake the memory of that night and every time we're around each other, I'm reminded of his hands on my body.

We haven't spoken about it, and I have a hard time reading him. He's been a perfect gentleman, hasn't made any kind of move since that night but sometimes I catch him looking at me and I think he's replaying the memory too. Maybe wishing it would happen again. It makes it hard for me to catch my breath.

There's a part of me that feels guilty for what happened between us, the part that still longs for Darren and my old life. But I haven't seen Darren in four months, haven't spoken to him in three. When I say it out loud to Lisa it doesn't seem like that much time but when you've lived it…under a second pandemic; well it feels like forever. If I keep holding on to my old life, how will I ever move forward in this one? And this one is all I have, all I can count on because from the look of things, America is only getting worse, not better and going home may never become an option.

Especially facing single parenthood, I need for look forward and I have to hold onto the friendships that I have so that's what I do. I put that night with Jack behind me and I lean into his friendship.

He is still trying to teach me how to cook but it's even more hopeless now that we move around the kitchen, desperately trying *not* to touch. Our conversation can be stilted when we're in such close proximity but it flows easily when we step outside the house and onto the beach or a trail. With the beautiful expanse of Hawaii laid out before us, we are distracted from the attraction between us.

Most days I follow him to the beach and sit in the sand reading while he surfs. I watch him in the ocean and wish I could feel that exhilaration again of the waves carrying me to shore but now that Jack knows about the baby, he won't let me surf as he thinks it's too dangerous.

When we aren't at the beach we're hiking and discovering new trails around the island. Our pocketbook of native Hawaiian plants is always tucked into the side pocket of Jack's backpack. When we find a new flower we fold that page in the book and these days it's looking pretty dog-eared. The hikes are harder now with my new body but I don't mind carrying my daughter with me.

What I do mind is the thought of going through labour. I'm so terrified of ruining my vagina, ripping right to my asshole or a future of peeing my pants that I can't sleep. Twice 've dreamed of delivering an actual watermelon and I don't wake up until after the nurse swaddles the melon and lays it in my arms. Lisa tries to tell me that my body was designed for this one task but I don't care – it still freaks me out. Enough of my friends have gone through labour and not one of them felt like their body was meant to do that.

30

SEPTEMBER 2023

Anna

Another month comes and goes and the night that Jack and I shared begins to fade and feel more like a dream than a memory. The sexual tension between us has lightened and we've returned to a comfortable friendship.

After an especially grueling hike today, we meander slowly through the neighbourhoods on our way back to Lisa's house. Many of the homes on this street are brightly coloured bungalows with exotic plants in their front gardens and old vehicles in the driveways. My heels are raw with blisters and I find myself wishing that we had driven to the trailhead instead of walked. My shoes are pinching, too tight now that my feet are starting to swell from the pregnancy.

I'm walking with my head down, staring at my feet as I focus on just putting one foot in front of the other when I realize that Jack's constant conversation has stopped. I look up to realize he is no longer beside me but a few houses back. He's browsing a garage sale on their front lawn. I sigh in frustration, wanting only to get home but I turn back to wait for him. That's when I notice a worn recliner on the lawn and I plop myself down in the chair, close my eyes and let him do his thing.

I reach down with one arm to find the wooden handle and I pop out the footrest, reclining fully and releasing a deep sigh. The relief my feet feel is inexplicable and with the warm sun on my face I think, I could totally nap here.

"Anna, wake up," Jack says a few minutes later, a hand on my shoulder to shake me awake.

"Mmmm?"

"Anna," I can hear Jack chuckling, "if you sleep any longer in this chair we're going to have to buy it."

"Ok, buy it," I say without opening my eyes.

"Ha!" He takes a look at the tag hanging off the side. "Actually, it's only twenty-five dollars, that's a pretty good deal. Think you can carry it?"

"I was only kidding," I say as I pop myself up to sitting and open my eyes. Jack is grinning at me. "Ready to go?"

"Ready." He reaches out a hand and helps me out of the chair and we head back down the street toward Lisa's.

"So what did you find today?" I ask, staring down at the white plastic bag he now carries.

He rummages through the bag and pulls the items out one by one. "Two new Nintendo games, another Harlequin romance novel for you, the guy on the cover looks like a total babe," he winks, "and this," he pulls out a small stuffed rabbit and hands it to me. The toy is soft and plush in my hands and I stroke one of the long ears. "I thought it might be good for the baby," Jack

151

says quietly. I'm instantly overcome with an image of a young girl, toddling around the house with one ear clutched in a tiny fist as the bunny drags behind her on the floor, her best friend that goes with her everywhere.

"I love it," I whisper, blinking furiously as tears threaten to fall.

"Good." I stop us in the middle of the sidewalk to pull him in for a hug.

Later that night, after we've eaten dinner, I'm lying on the couch with my new romance novel open in front of me and the stuffed bunny tucked under my arm. I'm doing everything I can to keep my eyes open even though I want nothing more than to crawl into bed but it's only 7pm. Jack sits on the other end of the couch and I've burrowed my feet under his thigh to keep them warm as I shiver in the frigid AC.

He's watching Lethal Weapon 3 with the volume low. A month or so ago Lisa found her ex-husband's old VCR and movie collection in the garage. Considering the relics we found in there, I think it's the first time she's cleaned it out since her ex moved out almost thirty years ago. Jack has been making his way through the collection of 80's and 90's action movies ever since.

He must notice me falling asleep because he tickles my ankle until my eyes flutter open. "Why don't you just go to bed," he asks.

"It's too early and I'm just getting to the good part," I respond, waving to the book.

"How can you read it if you can't keep your eyes open?"

"They're open," I mumble. Jack leans over and takes the book from me. "Why don't I read it to you and then you can go to bed?"

"Ok," I smile and half close my eyes. "Just start from the

top of the page."

Jack pauses the movie and starts reading. "Clara runs down the hill after Lorenzo and when she reaches him her large bosom is rising and falling heavily with her laboured breath. *What are you doing here*, Lorenzo asks angrily and Clara replies *I couldn't let you leave like that. What more is there to say?* He asks and Clara laments, *I wish I could marry you Lorenzo, but you know my father won't let me*."

Jack pauses and I catch him rolling his eyes. "You actually like this?"

"Shhh," I laugh. "Keep going."

"Lorenzo turns away from her and starts to walk away. *Lorenzo*, she cries, *don't leave me like this.* He whirls around angrily, *what more will you take from me, woman?* She runs to him and throws her arms around him, her bosom, straining against her tight bodice, is pressed to his chest. When she looks up at him she sees her own desire reflected in his eyes. Boldy, she stretches on her toes and kisses him. She can feel his swollen member thick against her thigh – wait, what is this?"

"The good part," I laugh. "You can't stop now!" Jack blushes but he continues reading and I can't keep the smile from my lips as I watch him staring intently at the page, not daring to meet my eyes as he reads through the lengthy and vivid sex scene.

31

OCTOBER 2023

DARREN

Anna's birthday is today. She'll turn thirty-three and I'll be thirty-five in December. October is her favourite month of the year, not just because a new year is beginning for her but also because she loves sweater weather and hiking through autumn leaves.

I somehow manage to get through the workday without thinking too much about her – about how I should have made her breakfast this morning and brought her flowers and undressed her slowly after dinner – but the empty house at night makes it impossible to avoid her. There are pictures and memories of us everywhere in this house. I haven't changed anything since I've been back. Maybe it's time I should. It's not like she's coming back.

I pick up a picture of Anna and I in a dark, walnut frame. There we are, standing on a mountain in Banff, completely innocent of what the future holds. I smash it on the floor. I look around me, at our faces smiling back at me, at the memories taunting me from the keepsakes and art we've brought into our home. I realize that I hate being here; I hate living with her ghost.

I leave the broken picture frame on the floor, the shards of glass catching light from the Edison bulbs of our black iron light fixture above me. I take the stairs two at a time and head to the bedroom where I quickly change into workout clothes. I hate running but the gyms are closed again, now that October has brought a second wave of infection and I can't stay here and keep breaking things. Slipping into a pair of old Nikes, I walk out the front door and set off at a sprint. My body complains almost instantly but I grit my teeth and keep running. I'm grateful for the painful sting of cold air into untrained lungs. The struggle to breathe makes it impossible to cry.

When I can't take it anymore, I slow to an even jog and start to take in my surroundings. The downtown core was just reaching peak gentrification in 2019 but suffered vastly from COVID-19 and again from C23 with forced closures. James St North is lined with boarded up doors – art galleries and restaurants and mom and pop shops. Signs of crime and homelessness have reappeared in the neighbourhood.

As my thoughts churn, I slow to a walk and give my legs some relief. I'll be plagued with shin splints tomorrow for sure. I take a moment to sit on a bench and catch my breath before walking the rest of the way home. The wind blows something colourful my way and I grab it on its way by. It looks like an old promo flyer for a nightclub and just as I'm about to crumple it up and throw it in the garbage, I catch the date. It's for tonight. Looking closer I realize it reads *FUCK COVID* at the top followed by *the government can't control us.* Looks like the old strip club on Barton St is having an unground party in defiance of local restrictions. At the bottom of the flyer it quotes Chuck Palahnuik, *'the first rule of Fight Club is: you do not talk about Fight Club.'* What better place to be when I feel as shitty as this?

32

OCTOBER 2023

DARREN

When I get home from my run, I grab a beer from the fridge and head straight to the shower. I manage to get a buzz going within the hour and just before midnight, I leave the house. Twenty minutes later I stand in front of the nightclub wearing dark jeans and a blue knit sweater. It's the nicest I've dressed in months considering Zoom calls don't even require pants.

The front of the building is deserted and for a moment I wonder if I got the date wrong but I head around back to see if there's another door. Walking through a parking lot full of broken glass and random garbage, I find a large metal door at the back of the building. I pound on it and a bouncer opens it quickly to lead me down a dimly lit hall. When we reach the main room, I take in the empty stripper poles gleaming under their spotlights. There is a long bar at the other end where only two people sit on ripped, leather stools.

"Where is everyone?" I ask the bouncer but he's already turned around and headed back down the hall. I can feel the thrum of heavy bass roll through my body starting from my feet but I can barely hear the music. I walk towards the bar and take a seat, ordering a straight bourbon from the bartender. When she returns with my drink, I repeat my earlier question. "Where is everyone?"

"In the basement. It's grotty down there but we can't play music up here. It would be heard on the street."

"Right." I down my drink in one go, enjoying the burn of the strong liquor, and she's already there with the bottle to refill my empty glass. I take in her features and feel desire creep across my skin. She's pale with long, black hair and green eyes like a cat. Her bow-shaped lips wear a bright red lipstick and I realize that it's the same shade that Anna wears.

The first time Anna and I hooked up she was wearing that lipstick. It was late and dark and we were a little bit drunk. Our mouths and hands were desperate, like we couldn't be together quick enough. When I woke up in the morning, I had red lip prints all over my body. And I want that tonight – no matter who they come from. Guilt burns my throat the same as the bourbon at the thought, so I grab my drink and turn away from the bartender. I head towards the door to the basement to find that it's nothing more than a cramped room with rough cinder block walls. The pounding music reverberates off of the low ceiling and strobe lights cast an eerie glow over the crowd of thrashing bodies. The air feels damp with sweat and desperation. *What the fuck am I doing here?*

I stay anyway and walk the outer edge of the crowd, not daring to enter the dance floor but afraid to go back to the bar and stare at those red lips. But before long, I drain the last dregs of bourbon from my glass and I'm forced to return to the other room.

My plan is to leave, to slide my glass onto the sticky bar top and walk out without another look but the thought of returning home to a house haunted by Anna makes me pause and gives the bartender enough time to ask, "another?" I sit down and she pours the amber liquid into my glass.

"I'm Lacey by the way." She sets the drink down in front of me. She's dressed in all black; a low-cut top with capped sleeves and ripped skinny jeans that show hints of smooth, porcelain skin.

"Darren."

"So, what's your story Darren?"

I shrug, not knowing what to say. "What's yours?"

"From Chicago, got stuck on this side of the border when the shitstorm landed."

"That must be hard, being away from home." I try desperately not to think of Anna.

"I'm just trying to survive. Not a lot of jobs for stranded foreigners, you know? But not everyone is following the rules and they're looking for people to take cash under the table. That's how I ended up here."

I look around me, "I haven't been here in years, not since my nineteenth birthday. My friends were going to buy me a lap dance but I was so drunk I was barely conscious. We were such jackasses back then."

"Who wasn't?" Lacey laughs. "God what I wouldn't give to be young again with no responsibilities."

"I'll cheers to that." I say casually but she takes it as an invitation and pours us both a shot of cheap tequila. I know from experience that tequila doesn't mix well with bourbon but I tap my glass to hers anyway and down it. I want to make poor decisions tonight, just like I did back then.

"Did you know this place use to be an old hotel? Like a hundred years ago."

"I had no idea."

"Yeah, rum-runners used it during prohibition apparently. There are tunnels all through this place and you would have seen the vault doors when you came in. Hamilton actually has a really cool past. There was this mobster, Rocco Perri, he was known as the 'King of the Bootleggers'."

"How do you know all this? I've lived in Hamilton my whole life and I don't know any of this."

"I found some old books upstairs. I'm living in one of the old hotel rooms. Anyone who works here is," she rushes to add. Her voice holds a hint of embarrassment. "Not a lot of options when you can't prove employment."

"I guess not. So, what other cool history can you tell me?"

"Well, there's a theory that Jack the Ripper used to live in Hamilton in the 1800's."

"No way."

"Yes way." Lacey says excitedly. She spends the next hour laying out the evidence of the notorious killer and filling up our shot glasses. By the time she asks me upstairs at the end of the night, I'm drunk enough to admit that I want this; that I want her.

She's nothing like Anna I think when we're upstairs, half out of our clothes. Not even the red lipstick looks the same in this light. I'm not sure if the dissimilarity is a good or bad thing but I know that I like the taste of tequila on her tongue. I like how she kneels before me to tug off my pants and leaves a hickey on my hip bone. Our sex is passionate and erotic and all kinds of things I shouldn't enjoy but I do. Afterwards, when she asks me to stay the night, I answer by pulling her tight against me. With my knees tucked in behind hers and an arm thrown across her middle, I sleep more soundly than I have in months.

In the morning, I wake to an empty bed and a terrible hangover. The rusty bedframe complains as I sit up in bed just as Lacey pads into the room on tiptoes with two steaming mugs of coffee. She's wearing a black lace thong and a tight tank top, no bra. My throat burns and I can't tell if it's acid reflux or guilt.

"That smells amazing," I say groggily.

"I thought you could use some."

"Thanks."

I take the cup she offers as she sits down next to me, slipping her legs back into the covers. We skip the small talk, choosing to sip our coffee in silence when it's time for me to leave, she watches me dress from her spot on the bed. I give her a chaste kiss on the cheek in parting and then I'm down the stairs and squinting into the bright sunlight.

I walk home slowly, noticing how different this part of town looks in the daylight. It's even sadder than it was at night; dirtier, more rundown. Kind of like my life.

33

OCTOBER 2023

DARREN

On the walk home I wait for the guilt to overpower me and shred me to pieces. But it doesn't cut like I want it to, the blade dull. I just cheated on my fiancé – didn't I? *Is* Anna my fiancé? Or is she a part of my past? Should I keep holding on to someone I might never see again?

After a shower, extra-strength Advil and two more coffees, I decide to visit Nat and confide in her what I've done. I don't bother texting her to say I'm coming over because I know she'll be home. With her due date a week away and severe cankles, she has no intention of leaving her house.

When she opens the door to me ten minutes later, I cross the threshold and walk in with my head down. "Hey, so I need your help. I've done something. Someone. Fuck, I can't believe I'm saying this – I slept with someone else. Someone who wasn't Anna. And I don't know how I'm supposed to feel about it."

"Uh huh," she grunts, "cool. Can we talk about this later?" *What the?* I snap my head up and look at her, confused. This is *not* the reaction I was expecting. Then I notice the look of distress on her face and how she's sucking in short breaths, and I think her pants are wet.

"What's wrong?"

"Oh nothing. I'm just in labour."

"What the fuck! Why aren't you at the hospital?"

"Well," she turns away from me and waddles to the nearest chair. "I kicked Chad out and I didn't think I should drive myself. I've been trying to reach him but he turned his phone off. Probably so I couldn't call and continue yelling at him, but it's been really inconvenient."

"I'm so confused, you kicked him out? What the hell happened?" Did he hit her? Did he cheat on her? Did he gamble away their money? Or take out loans behind her back?

"You wouldn't understand."

"Nat, if he hurt you," but she doesn't let me finish my train of thought.

"Oh my god, no! He put the toilet paper roll on wrong."

It takes me a second to digest her words but no, they still don't make sense. "What?"

"Ugh, my god, why are men so clueless? There's a right way and there's a *wrong* way to pull the roll on. And he put it on the *wrong* way."

"And this is why you kicked your husband out?"

"I told you, you wouldn't understand."

She's right – I don't. I just shake my head at her. "So, can I take you to the hospital now?"

"That's probably a good idea but…"

"But what?"

"Chad. I need him," she says and all of her bravado is gone and I can see how scared she is.

"Hey, you've got this," I crouch down to be on eye-level with her and I lay a hand on her arm. "You've already done it once before."

"Yeah, and it sucked!"

"Ok, fair. But I'll be with you until Chad gets there, ok?"

"Really? But the way you freaked out when I talked about mucus plugs…are you sure you're up for this?" I'm not but I don't say that.

"I'm sure. Let's go."

"Ok."

I help Nat to the car and once she's buckled into the front seat, I run back into the house and look for the hospital bag while also dialling Chad at the same time. With the phone cradled between my cheek and shoulder, I run upstairs and find the bag in their bedroom. I leave a voicemail for Chad and at the last second, write a note that I stick to the front door on my way out, *baby is coming, meet us at the hospital.*

By the time I slide into the driver's seat Nat has entered panic mode. She's dialling Chad over and over again to no avail. I start backing out of the driveway but slam on the brakes in my own fit of panic.

"Oh my god, where's Logan? I forgot your son!" I shout, throwing the car into park. I'm halfway out the door when Nat grabs a fistful of my shirt and pulls me back in.

"He's at my mom's. He goes every Saturday."

"Oh, thank god." I lay my head on the steering wheel for a minute before closing my door and pulling out of the driveway.

When we arrive at the hospital, everything seems to happen very fast. We're given a room and a nurse is asking Nat a bunch of questions. Everyone is in PPE and they look like astronauts, it's incredibly unsettling.

I look away as Nat lays back and the nurse reaches into her gown to check her dilation. Nat is asking how quickly she can get the epidural but the nurse is being evasive and telling us to wait for the doctor. Shortly after she leaves, the doctor enters the room and tells us that Nat needs a C-section immediately. The doctor explains the procedure but Nat is looking at me shaking her head. I grab her hand and tell her she can do this.

"I want Chad," she whispers and I'm only mildly offended.

"Pfft, the guy who can't even put toilet paper on right? Come on." She laughs through her tears and grips my hand tighter. I don't let go the whole way to the operating room.

In less than ten minutes we are robed and the procedure is under way. I stand above the raised curtain, holding Nat's hand and talking nonsense, anything to keep her distracted. In no time at all the baby is out and they hand him to me.

"He's got Chad's mustache!" I joke and Nat starts crying immediately. "I was just kidding! No facial hair, I promise." I crouch down so Nat can be eye to eye with her newborn son and she reaches out a finger that he grasps in his tiny hand.

The nurse helps to pull Nat's gown down over her shoulders and lays the baby on her bare chest for skin-to-skin contact. Just then the door of the operating room bursts open and there's Chad, half in and half out of the blue hospital gown, rushing to Nat's side. I watch him bend down to kiss her, whispering apologies, before laying a delicate kiss on the head of his son. I take a step back and stare at the family in front of me. I think of Anna and I wish it was *us*, kissing and whispering over our newborn baby. I wish it was us, I wish it was me, I wish it was ours.

Nat looks up at me and seems to read my thoughts. "Don't give up hope Darren, she's coming back to us." I smile at her and rub my eyes so the tears don't fall.

A short while later when Nat and the baby are settled back in their room, I make to leave. "Well, you probably want some rest, so I'll leave you to it. Just call me if you need anything."

"Darren, I can't thank you enough for being here," Nat stretches out a hand from the bed and I squeeze it.

"Of course."

"Yeah, thanks man," Chad says, slapping me on the back.

"Seriously, I couldn't have done it without you. Anna would be so proud of you."

"Nat I..." I want to tell her about last night, I want her to reassure me that I haven't completely fucked everything up. Especially now that I know what I want; that I can give Anna everything she's asking for.

"What is it?"

"I slept with someone. Last night."

"What?!" Her voice rises multiple octaves and she hands the baby to Chad. "Tell. Me. Everything."

"It's what I was saying when I came over."

"Yeah, I didn't take in a single word." So I fill her in with sparing details about the night and try to lay out my confusing mass of feelings. "I'm a mess Nat. I'm a fucking mess."

34

NOVEMBER 2023

Anna

Jack and I are sitting on the floor of my old room – the garden suite that I once shared with Darren. God, I can't believe that was eight months ago; sometimes it feels like yesterday and sometimes it feels like a lifetime.

I don't like being detached from the main house but it's the biggest room and the baby and I will need the space. The memories of Darren are still here but they're faded. When they surface I try not to ignore them but simply acknowledge them and let them pass. *God, I'm starting to sound like Jerry,* I think, and I feel a twinge of regret that I haven't seen him in awhile. I miss our sessions together but he doesn't think I need them anymore. Can't we just hang out, I asked him.

Jack and I sit on the soft cream carpet with pieces of a disassembled crib all around us. A soft stream of sunlight falls across us, and I think about how I'd probably be watching the first snowfall if I was back home. I shiver involuntarily as if I can feel the cold air on the nape of the neck, beckoning winter into being.

"Fuck!" Jack shouts, pulling me from my reverie.

"What?!"

"Sorry, it's nothing," he says sheepishly. I watch as he takes a hammer to a screw.

Jack is trying to assemble the crib and needless to say, it's not going as planned. I can't do much with this large belly of mine so I sit here cross-legged, folding newly washed baby clothes and watching him struggle. Jack found the crib at a garage sale of course. I was with him, searching through a bin of toys when he stumbled across it at the curb. The owner was going to throw it out thinking no one would want to put it together without the instructions which were long gone but Jack insisted that he could. I'm not so sure he can.

"I'm no handyman but I'm pretty sure you don't hammer screws."

"It's stripped," he says as he drops the hammer and picks up the screwdriver again. With gritted teeth he applies his weight to the screwdriver but the screw spins uselessly in the hole, not digging into the wood.

"Can we get another screw? Or drill a new hole?"

He chucks the screwdriver back into the toolbox in frustration. "I'll figure something out."

"Ok," I say, turning back to my pile of baby clothes. If Nat were here, we would have a good laugh at male stubbornness right now. God how I wish she was here. There are so many things I want to ask her about! Like why did my nipples turn so brown and why is my crotch on fire all the time and what if I don't get any of this parenting thing right? I also want to know how she's doing and what life is like for her and if she's had her new baby yet. Is Logan adjusting to being a big brother, was Chad able to keep his bar open and what has he done recently to piss her off?

I want to tell her about Jack and how my feelings for him have only grown since that night we shared. I want to tell her how badly I want him and how confused it makes me - I'm pregnant with another man's baby and that man was the love of my life. But Darren feels more and more like a character from a novel that I once read while Jack is right here, right in front of me and he makes me feel alive in a time of so much death.

It's almost unbelievable when I think of the time that has passed since Nat and I last talked. We've been best friends since high school and I can't think of a time where we went more than a few days without a call or a text. But time is a funny thing under lockdown. One day bleeds into the next and the next. If it weren't for my growing belly, I don't think I'd be able to say how many months had passed. It could have been 2 months or 2 years. It's almost funny how much significance I put on *time* when it came to my relationship with Darren. Time means nothing to me now.

The room has fallen silent and I look over to Jack and he is standing by the completed crib.

"It's done," I exclaim with a smile. He turns to me and offers a hand to help me up from the floor. "Do you think it will stay together?"

"Probably going to collapse the first time you put her in it," he laughs and I smack his arm playfully. "Ow! I was just kidding."

"I love it," I say, sliding my hands across the wood that has been worn smooth by generations of tiny hands. "Thank you."

"I can't wait to meet her," Jack says so quietly I almost don't hear it. I can't help myself, I stand on tippy-toes and kiss him on the mouth.

35

NOVEMBER 2023

Anna

I'm asleep on the couch when I awaken to Jack tickling my feet. "Bedtime?"

I mumble groggily in reply. I blink my eyes open and see that the movie credits are running. Tonight we watched Indiana Jones and I'm kind of bummed that I missed the second half of the movie. I was enjoying it. I want to ask how it ended but all that comes out is "mmm, bed."

Jack has been sleeping in my room the last few nights. There's hardly been more than two inches between us at any given time since we kissed a few days ago. But every time he makes a move for sex, I pretend to be asleep (which isn't hard to do considering how tired I am in my third trimester). It's not because I don't want to have sex – I really, really do – but not in this large, pregnant body.

"Don't wake up, I'll carry you," Jack says, getting up from

the couch.

"Jack, no," I say, trying to bury myself deeper into the couch. "I'm too big. I'm too heavy."

"You're not," he slips his arms under me but I quickly bounce up onto my feet.

"I am."

Jack lightly grabs my wrist as I skate around him. "Do I need to show you? Just how *not heavy* you are?" He says and I immediately feel a heat spreading up my neck. "Because I can do that. I can show you just how light you are." He pulls me to him and lays an erotic kiss at the base of my neck where it meets my collarbone. Like it's nothing, Jack slips his arms under my legs and lifts me into the air. I'm laughing at the ridiculousness of it all as he carries me to my room.

"Now do you believe me?" He asks as he lays me on the bed and all I can do is nod, my throat thick with desire. We've been waiting for this for months and with an undeniable hunger, his mouth devours mine, his tongue searching and exploring. He eases himself along side of me and trails kisses down my neck to my chest. I am sliding out of my pants as fast as I possibly can, while he kisses me, desperate to have him but Jack is taking his time. I've yanked my tank top over my head and thrown my bra across the room but still, he doesn't undress.

"Jack," I beg, a whisper on bated breath.

He sits back on his knees and runs his eyes up and down my exposed body. My chest is rising and falling quickly with my need for him. "You know you're beautiful right?"

"Show me." He falls on me with a new urgency, slipping inside me swiftly, claiming my mouth, my body and afterwards, he pulls me into his arms before I can even think about getting dressed. We talk for hours, letting the night pass gently by us and all the while, he touches my body – gentle strokes and caresses down my arms and back and belly. I start to believe that this body is beautiful.

36

DECEMBER 2023

Anna

My due date is fast approaching and I'm having trouble sleeping. I'm plagued with nightmares where I pee my pants in all kinds of public scenarios. How many women lose control of their bladders after giving birth? I would Google it if I could. In hopes of giving me a dream-free sleep and also because I'm just too tired to focus, Jack has taken up reading my romance novels to me before bed.

Tonight, I'm curled up under the covers, eyelids droopy with sleep while Jack sits stretched out on top of the duvet with his back resting against the headboard.

"Scarlet is walking through the forest," he reads, "when she comes upon Vince and Amelia in the meadow. She takes cover behind a tree and watches the man she thought she loved bend down to lay a gentle kiss on the lips of another woman. Scarlet gasps and Vince turns his head at the sound, catching sight of

Scarlet at the edge of the clearing. *Sccrlet,* Vince shouts after her as she turns and runs. *It's not what you think* but his words are whipped away by the wind – ok well that's bullshit," Jack says, "how is it not what it looks like? He's making out with some other chick in the forest."

I can't help but laugh at Jack's commentary. "I love that you're so protective of Scarlet."

"Vince is a dick, she can do so much better."

"Remember when you first started reading to me? You thought these books were ridiculous."

"Oh, I still do."

"You love them, just admit it."

"I love *you*, that's why I read them."

"I love you too," I say, snuggling up to him. The moment is casual despite the fact that this is the first time we've said it to each other. Maybe because it comes so easily or maybe because we've been in love for months, but we don't need to make it a grand declaration. It's always been known.

37

Anna

My daughter arrives on a Friday night just before midnight in an anxious rush to meet the world. I deliver at the local health clinic, a swarm of friendly nurses around me. With C23 cases at an all time low, they allow both Lisa and Jack to be in the room with me. Lisa paces at my feet issuing instructions like a coach while Jack stays silent, standing at my shoulder with his palm firmly in mine.

For hours I try to endure the pain but I eventually cave and take the epidural. I almost back out when I have to sign a waiver with terrifying potential side effects such as paralysis, but I scribble my name quickly when another contraction comes on.

There's an ease and calm that creeps in once I've had some relief from the epidural. I even manage to get a few fitful hours of sleep. When it's time to push, there's a stinging burn between my legs as my daughter crowns and all of a sudden her screams are there, matching my own. They place her on my chest immediately and I dip my head to hers, smelling her scent, tinged with blood.

After so much fear of ripping during delivery, I don't even know if it happened. If it did, I didn't feel it. Instead I felt powerful as she slipped from my body and now I am too consumed by my daughter to notice what the nurses are doing to clean me up.

When everything is quieter, Lisa lays a hand on the crown of my daughter's head and says, "congratulations, she's beautiful."

I look up at her, "I'd like to name her Kaila, after your daughter, if that's ok." I see Lisa's eyes fill with tears and I hurry to explain myself, "it's just that you've been like a mother to me, and I wanted to honour you and your daughter but if I'm crossing a line, just say so."

"Oh honey, no, I'd be honoured. It's such a beautiful name," and she kisses Kaila on the head. Jack squeeze's my shoulder and I take some comfort in the love that surrounds me but it feels like something is missing. I long for Nat and her brazen humour, I long for my Mom and the peace her presence used to give me, and a piece of me – a deep, buried piece of me wishes that Darren were here to welcome his daughter into the world, to tell me that he forgives me, to tell me that he loves me.

38

DECEMBER 2023

Anna

It's New Years Eve and our little house of four is having a party. We've gorged ourselves on sashimi all night long as is a Hawaiian tradition on New Years Eve.

Two hours ago we stood outside in the street beneath an ink black sky and waved to our neighbours as bright fireworks exploded in the distance. No one bothered with masks – it's more common now that the C23 case count is declining - and it was beautiful to witness everyone's smiles lit up by the sparklers in their hands and the hope of a new year.

Tonight I had my first drink since finding out I was pregnant – champagne; my own New Years tradition. Nat and I always have a bottle of champagne on New Years. We don't bother with glasses but drink straight from the bottle, passing it back and forth between us. How is she celebrating this year? Does she feel an empty space beside her where I'm supposed to be?

I tip the bottle back and take a sip, basking in the feeling of the soft bubbles rolling across my tongue.

I hear my daughter crying on the monitor and I slip away from the celebrations, grabbing a bottle of pre-pumped milk from the fridge as I pass. It's still so strange for me to think *my daughter*; I'm someone's *mother* and completely responsible for keeping them alive. It's been wonderful and terrifying and overwhelming, but I think I'm getting the hang of it.

I pick Kaila up and we settle in the glider. These times are my favourite, when we sit silently together and she looks up at me like I'm the only thing in the world. I witnessed this bond so often between my friends and their newborns and I wanted it desperately.

Even despite the fear of sacrificing my body, my time, my energy, my mental and emotional capacity, I wanted this. For years I suffered through intense jealousy towards those who had it and resentment towards Darren for making me feel like I had to choose it or him – a baby or Darren. It was lonely, facing this huge life decision – do I end it, do I leave him? Do I wait; for how long? In the end it didn't really matter, did it? All that worrying for nothing.

Darren is on my mind so much more now that I have Kaila. She gives me a wide-eyed look as she drinks and I remember a night with Darren, dancing in the glowing moonlight that fell through our front window. An Aerosmith vinyl was playing and Darren was more than a little drunk. He gave me an intense stare that made me laugh and ask *"what?"* and he said, *"I hope our kids get your eyes."*

I savoured that moment. I held it like a treasure every time I doubted him, every time I thought about leaving him, every time I thought I couldn't live without a baby. Maybe he couldn't tell me when he would be ready but at least I knew he wanted them, and he wanted them with me.

In the end though, Darren's wish didn't come true because she has *his* eyes – wide and grey and thickly lashed. I know they won't change because the gold starburst around her pupil is an exact match to her Dad's. She does have my feathery blonde hair though and my dimple too. It's so much cuter on her.

I stroke her cheek as her eyes close and belly becomes full. "We made something beautiful, Darren," I whisper into the night and I let the tears fall, crying for what could have been.

39

JANUARY 2024

DARREN

It's New Year's Eve or I guess technically New Year's Day now and as much as I wanted to spend the evening alone, I'm glad to be surrounded by family.

I stand outside on the porch of our rented chalet in the Blue Mountains of Collingwood and smoke a joint.   I'm hoping my Dad doesn't walk out here and catch me. Even though I'm an adult and weed is legal, I still feel like a teenager who has to sneak around. The night is dark except for the lit tip of my joint and the weak lamp light falling through the windows. In the darkness I can see snowflakes falling softly all around me. They coat the ground in white.

The family and I have been up here since Christmas Eve and I almost turned my car around the moment I pulled in. My parents were standing on the porch waving at me, the other arm wrapped around each other's waist. They were wearing matching Christmas sweaters and I wondered what kind of Christmas movie hell was I walking into.

Hallmark movie level it turned out. When I entered the house I was hit with the scent of freshly baked cookies, the sounds of excited children and a ten foot tall Christmas tree. My sister was in the kitchen, oven mitts on her hands, while her two kids were under the Christmas tree, shaking the wrapped presents.

Alicia ran over to me and hugged me for a good four minutes, whispering in my ear just how sorry she was that Anna wasn't here. I was afraid to come here and suffer her pity. Just as I was afraid to watch her happy family. I didn't want to be with family because I knew there would be a gaping hole where Anna should be. But with each passing day this week it became easier. I forgot how much fun Alicia and I had together, how good it was to reminisce about our childhood. Her kids love hearing about their mom as a kid and I love telling embarrassing stories about her.

I turn around and look through the window into the living room as I take another pull on my joint, coughing a little on the hot smoke. The clock has already struck twelve and the kids have gone to bed. The bottle of champagne sits empty on the coffee table surrounded by half-drunk glasses. My parents are sitting on the couch and it looks like my mom might be asleep, her head on Dad's shoulder. Alicia and her husband sit on the floor playing a game of cards and she swats his arm playfully before leaning over and giving him a kiss.

I thought being around them would make me feel lonelier, that their happiness would remind me of everything that I had lost. But what I thought would hurt has actually healed.

They've reminded me of why I want Anna back so badly and

being with them has solidified what I felt when I stood next to Nat as she gave birth – I'm ready for a family. Desperate even. On instinct, I pull out my phone and text Anna. I know she'll never get it, there's a long list of messages in blue bubbles that she'll never get, but I do it anyway. It's a small way that I can feel some kind of connection to her and I need to keep the hope alive that I'll get her back. Sooner rather than later, I hope.

D: we're going to make beautiful babies together and I can't wait 🖤

40

FEBRUARY 2024

Anna

Babies are great and wonderful and amazing and I *love* my daughter but anyone who says that *every* single moment is cherishable is a straight up liar.

Today is one of the bad days; most of our days are good days, Kaila and I having slipped into an easy routine these past two months but today nothing I do seems right. I change her, I feed her, I cuddle her but she won't stop crying no matter what. Her wide, toothless wails and fat, wet tears are absolutely heart-wrenching. Every fibre of my being is screaming at me to fix this but I can't and that has lead me to a whole new level of anxiety.

I reflect on all the time I spent wishing for a baby, on the hopelessness I felt every month when I saw a slick of blood on the toilet paper. I never did picture the hard parts of motherhood.

I swaddle Kaila and hold her to my chest, swaying and rubbing her back but she just continues to cry. She cries so hard that she vomits all over me and that gets me crying too. All I want to do is fix this for her.

Lisa walks into my room at that moment, "I heard you from the house and wondered if I could help." I just want to hug her but I'm covered in vomit.

"I don't know what she needs, she just won't stop crying."

"Oh baby," she coos as she reaches for Kaila and takes her from me. "Sometimes they just won't be soothed. Why don't you leave her with me and take a moment to relax. My yoga mat is set up on the deck if you want to do some flows."

"Thanks Lisa." I wipe my tears and pull off my puke-stained shirt, using the inside to wipe any puke off of my neck and shoulder and then slip into a clean one.

I head to the main house and find Lisa's yoga mat in a swath of sunshine on the porch. I fall, cross-legged, onto the middle of the mat and take a few deep breaths. For a brief moment I picture Jerry as he was in our first session, rolling on the floor in happy baby pose and I can't help but laugh.

I fall onto my back with my legs wide and my arms at my sides in savasana. I try to focus on slowing and deepening my breath but I'm having a hard time blocking out the screeching wails of my daughter. After ten minutes of trying I accept that I'm not going to find any peace today and I make my way back to Lisa and Kaila.

"It's going to get better," Lisa says as if she can read my mind.

"I know," I say, smiling weakly.

That night, after endless hours of crying, I finally get Kaila to sleep by singing her Aerosmith's *I Don't Want To Miss A Thing*. I knew singing *our* song would bring back painful memories – like kissing in the car at red lights whenever the song comes on or finding each other across the room whenever the song is played at a wedding – but I can handle memories of Darren if it puts Kaila to sleep.

I tip-toe over to the bed where Jack is waiting for me. It looks like he's fallen asleep already, our latest romance novel open on his bare chest. I pull off my shirt and my nursing bra, wincing as the fabric scrapes my nipples. They're raw and sore AF and I wonder if I'll ever let Jack touch them again. I fall into bed next to him and am asleep in seconds.

What feels like only a minute later, Jack is nudging me awake from a blurry dream about Darren. Or was it a memory?

"What is it?" I mumble, refusing to open my eyes.

"Kaila's fussing. I think she might be hungry."

Just the thought of her mouth on my sore nipples makes my eyes well with tears.

"What's wrong?"

"I can't, Jack."

"What do you mean?"

"I can't feed her. It's too much. I need to sleep."

"I know it must feel all consuming right now but it'll get better. Before you know it, she'll be a moody teenager that won't even want to talk to you?"

"Do you promise?" I ask tearily.

"Promise," he says with a kiss. Kaila's snuffling turns into full on wailing and everything inside me winces. I start crying myself.

"Jack, I can't do this."

"You can. You're superwoman."

"No, I'm just me. I'm just a regular woman."

"I don't know what you want me to say."

"I don't want you to *say* anything, I want you to *do* something."

"But you've got the boobs."

"Please, Jack, just figure it out."

"But…no, you're right, I can figure this out. Go back to sleep." He gives me a kiss as I fall back into the pillows. I don't know how my Mom ever did this on her own.

When I wake in the morning it's to an empty bed. I feel relaxed and refreshed for the first time in months. The bedside clock says 6:32am as I slip out of bed and pad quietly to the crib to check on Kaila but the crib is empty. There's a slight panic in my chest as I slip on my sandals and run through the fog and drizzle of a gloomy morning to the main house. When I burst through the back sliding door, I realize that I had nothing to worry about.

Jack and Kaila are sound asleep on the living room couch, Kaila lying flat on Jack's chest, her little head tucked under his chin. There's a half-drunk bottle on the floor beside the couch and an open can of formula and Lisa's car keys on the kitchen counter. He figured it out. A wave of love so intense washes over me, I can barely stand it. I want to stand here and stare at them forever but I know I should take this opportunity to shower – I don't get many chances these days. I slip silently out the door, leaving them both to sleep.

Back in my own room, I step out of my pajamas which smell like sour milk and turn the shower on hot. I stand beneath the powerful blast of hot water and nothing has ever felt so good. I take my time, scrubbing my hair vigorously and breathing in the scent of my shampoo. I use the last squirt of my expensive, rose scented bodywash that I brought with me on my vacation so long ago and for a moment I feel like me again. Not a mother, just Anna.

It feels luxurious to have time, to let my hands linger over my body instead of quickly scrubbing, peeking out a partially open curtain to keep an eye on my daughter. It feels good to be touched gently (even if it is just me) instead of pinched, punched, or tugged. I think about letting Jack touch me like this again sometime soon and it excites me.

I pull the showerhead down and hold it close to my skin as I rinse the soap away. I pause between my legs, letting the water caress me and I can feel pressure building. I picture an old memory, of a similarly gloomy morning, of Darren coming up behind me in the bathroom as I undressed to shower. How he laid kisses all the way down my spine, how I turned in his arms and brought his mouth to mine, how he lifted me up to the bathroom counter, how the rain pattered on the skylight above us, how the mirror fogged from our breathing, how I shook with pleasure, like how I shake now.

PART THREE

Spring

2024

41

MAY 2024

Anna

The United States turns right side up just as quickly as it turned upside down. Within weeks of the CDC declaring that the country is now in the endemic stage of the virus, any remaining lockdown restrictions are lifted and the President promises to restore the internet and cell service within the month. World leaders are in discussions to re-open their borders to stranded citizens and for the first time in a long time I start to believe that going home is actually a possibility. But do I *want* to go home? I don't know.

Jack and I mostly avoid talking about it and it's created tension between us. What will it mean for us? Something else I don't know. To date, our relationship has come with an incredible ease, but we've been living outside the bounds of normal life and now our old responsibilities have come knocking at the door. But I don't want to think about any of this tonight because tonight, the island is celebrating.

With Lisa watching Kaila for me, I take my time getting ready, even taking the opportunity to shave my legs and apply expensive lotion. I curl my hair and then brush it out until I have silky, soft waves. I swipe my eyelashes with mascara and my lips with a nude lipstick. I dress in a flowy maxi dress patterned with soft yellow flowers and slip my feet into wedge sandals. Kaila wears a frilly romper in the same pattern as my dress and a yellow bow on her bald head.

"Don't my girls look beautiful tonight," Jack says when he sees us, wrapping us both up in a giant hug. I can't help but smile.

The town is having a Luau to celebrate the country returning to some semblance of normal and when we arrive it feels like the whole island is here. There are bonfires on the beach and tables upon tables of food and flowers floating in the Mai-Tai's. Everyone has a sweet-smelling lei to accentuate their outfit and every single person wears a smile, including me.

I find the crowd overwhelming at first after so many months of wearing masks and social distancing. I keep to Lisa's side like a shy child as she introduces us. I've met a lot of people during my year here through garage saleing and shopping at the markets but with the pandemic, social distancing and masks, I didn't get to develop many deep friendships. But it doesn't feel like that tonight because everyone embraces me like they're greeting a long-lost friend and I'm reminded by how much I love this place. *Home* seems incredibly distant.

I'm hugged tightly by a short, stout Hawaiian woman with long jet-black hair. "This must be the little baby who loved papaya so much," she says as she touches the tip of my daughter's nose. The woman looks vaguely familiar but I can't place her. When she sees my confused expression, she laughs. "You probably don't recognize me without my mask! I own the fruit stand at the market, you were always craving papaya when you were pregnant."

"Of course!" I exclaim, laughing and pulling her back into another hug. "This is Kaila," I say, hitching her up higher on my hip.

"Hi Kaila, you little papaya baby, nice to meet you." Kaila gurgles back happily. Looking back up to me the woman gives me a smile and blows Kaila a kiss before turning away to welcome other friends.

I feel a tap on my shoulder and I turn around to find Jerry's wide smile and he pulls me into a tight embrace. When he pulls back he pauses for a moment taking in my bright smile. "You look good," he says and I know he's not talking about my dress or my hair or my makeup. I can feel my eyes start to tear up as I think about how far I've come and Jerry pulls me back in for another tight squeeze. I introduce him to Kaila and look around for Jack who is fully engrossed in a conversation with another couple I don't recognize. I point him out to Jerry and promise to introduce them later and then before I know it, Lisa is ushering me to our table.

The show begins while we eat and dancers appear to the steady beat of a drum. It is unlike anything I have ever seen before. I revel in the pound of the panu drums, the soft swish of the dancer's skirts and the silence of their feet in the sand as they dance. They tell stories of the island, of creation, of legend.

Once the show is over, the drummers switch to a soft beat and the crowd rises to their feet. Some people drift off to stand at the bonfires and watch the sun set over the ocean but most grab a partner and dance in the fading twilight. Jack turns to me, palm outstretched. I look to Lisa who is rocking Kaila into a soft sleep and she gives me an easy smile that says *go ahead, I've got her*. How would I do any of this without her? Without Jack? We've become a family here and I don't want that to lose that, but change is on the horizon and I can't say for certain what is going to happen. But tonight, I will dance with the man that I love, the one that is here and I will be *present,* not thinking of tomorrow and not of yesterday. I put my hand in Jack's and let him lead me to the dance floor.

By the time we leave the party the sun has set and a full moon has risen, lighting the walk home. I feel alive and happy and like I've made a hundred new friends tonight. Kaila is asleep and heavy in my arms and my body is tired from all the dancing and laughing. Lisa and Jack talk quietly as we make our way to the house. In our room, I lay Kaila in her crib and then I let Jack slide my dress down my body until it pools on the floor. He pulls me close but even when he's inside me, it isn't close enough. I want to crawl into his skin and co-exist.

42

MAY 2024

Anna

I'm home alone with Kaila this afternoon. Jack is out surfing and Lisa is at the farmer's market. Kaila and I are in the living room. I sit on the floor with my back resting against the couch as I watch Kaila on a blanket in front of me practicing tummy time. The news is on the TV, the volume low and muffled. We've had it on constantly since the endemic announcement, waiting for the day the news anchors tell us we can go home.

I catch the words cell service and internet and I snap my head up to find a red BREAKING NEWS banner. I turn the volume up and listen, my face slack with shock, as they confirm that internet and cell phone service has just been restored across the country. *Nat.*

I drop the remote and reach into my back pocket for my phone but it isn't there. I don't see it on the coffee table either or on the floor so I lean forward and slip my hands under the blanket that Kaila is on wondering if it's underneath. I run my hands over the plush carpet but I don't feel anything. I tickle Kaila from under the blanket until she giggles. All of a sudden I hear the chime of a text message from somewhere behind me. Adrenaline and anxiety both dump into my veins and make my hands shaky. I turn to the couch and search between the cushions but there's only small coins and crumbs. I slam my face into the soft microfibre of the cushion. Ugh, where the hell is it? I lift my head when I hear another chime – it's coming from the kitchen. I find my phone on the island and I stare at the black screen almost afraid to touch it. All this time it has been nothing more than a glorified camera and iPod to me. I keep one eye on Kaila and one eye on the phone as I stand here, hesitant. And then the screen lights up with another text. *Nat.*

I swipe up on the phone but it won't unlock with the FaceID and asks me for my passcode. It takes me three tries to get it right because my hands are so shaky. I go to open my texts but I receive a pop-up notification telling me I must agree to the new Terms of Service. Blindly, I hit agree. I'll learn later that I agreed to allow the government all access to my data and I understood that the spread of misinformation would be prosecuted and subject to a jail sentence. I'll be appalled when I learn this but it's not like I had a choice. No agreement, no service, no internet, no Nat.

I'm finally able to open my texts and I find a few from her that are old, sent when the network went down. I guess they got stuck and are now just delivering. I'm surprised they didn't just disappear.

N: Chad is complaining that I'm always tired and never want to do anything. I'm PREGNANT Chad

N: AND I have a toddler. Of course all I want to do is sleep. Men.

N: Why aren't my messages delivering?

N: Are you getting my messages?

N: Is this really happening?

And then a message from today comes in.

N: Anna?

N: omg it shows as delivered 🙌

N: I love you, I miss you, call me call me call me!!

Her last message makes me laugh and cry at the same time. I start dialing her number, I can't wait to hear her voice but… how do I even begin to explain what happened? I look up at Kaila who's fallen asleep on her blanket; how do I tell Nat that I had a baby? She never even knew I was pregnant. How do I tell her everything else – that the depression came back worse than before; that I fell in love; that I've changed. How do I tell her that I miss her but that I'm afraid to come home? I delete the numbers that I've pressed and lock the phone. I walk back to the couch and take up my spot next to Kaila. I rub her back as it rises and falls slowly with her breath. I wish I could sleep as soundly as she does. I've set my phone on the coffee table and it chimes again, the screen glowing. I imagine it's Nat saying, *why aren't you calling me?* I ignore it. Another chime and then another. I flip the silence switch and turn it upside down without looking at the screen. I don't want to see her name there, staring back at me.

The phone vibrates with another text and it keeps vibrating. It's vibrating so much it's edging off the table. Kaila grunts and rolls in her sleep and I worry the constant vibrations against the wood will wake her so I finally pick up the phone. I'll just send Nat a quick text telling her that I'll call her later. But when I look at the screen it's not Nat, it's Darren and the messages keep coming in. The count beneath his name just keeps rising until it reads over 365 texts. A year's worth.

I am crying again before I even read them, crying more as I go through each and every one. My nose is running fiercely but I don't bother to grab a tissue, I'm stuck in place, riveted to the floor. My heart breaks as I read through his messages, his feelings, his days, his hopes, his fears. Some messages stand out more than others.

D: I love you

D: I miss you

D: I'm going to find a way to fix this

D: How do you get Nat to stop talking? She's talking about a mucus plug and I want it to stop...

I laugh, it's so like Nat to overshare.

D: I never should have left you

D: I ordered tacos from our favourite place but it's just not the same without you

I can picture the restaurant, the back wall lined with hundreds of bottles of tequila and by the door, large paintings from Mexican artists; booths with brightly printed pillows to lean into and high bar tables with unlevel chairs. The tacos are out of this world.

D: this bed is so empty without you

D: do you remember that red dress you wore in Paris? Fuck you were so beautiful.

D: Nat misses you like crazy. Almost as much as I miss you

D: Nat is making me watch 90 day fiancé how do you guys

like this stuff?

D: well Megan and Daryl definitely shouldn't be together… what is she thinking? #90dayfail

D: Nat has been telling me hilarious stories of your high-school days…I think she's going to pull out some old pictures soon

D: Facebook is a treasure trove. Full of hidden gems

D: and to think of how much you made fun of my hair in my old prom photo lmao 😄

D: I feel so alone

D: I dreamt about you last night. I never wanted to wake up.

I lay a hand over my heart as I take in months worth of messages filled with hopelessness and despair.

D: it feels like you're never coming home.

D: this is all my fault

D: I slept with someone. It felt terrible but also good. I wanted her to be you, but she wasn't. No one is. But I don't think I can be alone forever.

When I read this last message I have to stop, it hits me like a punch to the gut. I want to be sick at the thought of him being with someone else, touching someone else, kissing them, telling them he loves them. It's not fair for me to feel betrayed considering I've done all the same but a small part of me still does. Who is she? I want to call Nat and stalk her on Instagram and have Nat tell me I'm prettier and Darren's an idiot. Another part of me though hopes that he found some comfort in this woman; but not too much. I keep reading.

D: I shouldn't have sent that. What if you get these messages someday? I'd rather confess in person. Fuck. She was no one, I promise. It won't happen again.

D: Nat had a son; I was with her. Did you know there's a wrong way to put the toilet paper roll on? Anyway, he's beautiful, she's beautiful. They make me hopeful again.

D: I'm going to bring you home.

D: Happy New Years my love

D: we're going to make beautiful babies together and I can't wait 🖤

D: Anna, I hope that one day I get to tell you this in person but for my own sanity, I need to get it out now. I'm sorry that I made you wait for a wedding and a baby when you wanted both so badly. I know it hurt you and made you question my love for you but it was never that. I've always loved you. I wish you could have had more confidence in that. I wish I could have given you more of a say in the decision but if I wasn't ready, what else was there to do? As much as it hurt you and as much as I never wanted to hurt you, I still think it was the right thing to do. I think I would have let you down if we'd rushed into things too soon. And now we're apart. Just when everything feels right, just when I feel ready for it all. You might say I've come down with baby fever lol. It started when Nat's son was born, when I helped her bring him into the world. All I wanted was for it to be you, to be our child. This feeling of 'rightness' that I was waiting for, it's here and it grows every day. I see the families around me and I want nothing more than to build that with you. I want you, all of you. I want to marry you and put a baby in you (hope that doesn't sound gross lol) and I want to grow old with you and meet our grandchildren with you. I want you. So when you come home, and you will, you have to, I'm going to give you the life you've always dreamed of.

I'm sobbing – can't breath, can't open my eyes, snot dripping kind of sobbing. It's woken Kaila but I don't reach for her, I just hunch over myself and sob and Darren's words run through my mind in a loop. My crying is so loud that I don't hear the front door when Jack comes in but I jump in surprise when he lays a hand on my shoulder and I involuntarily chuck my phone onto the floor.

"Anna, what's wrong?"

"The phones are back," I say, collecting myself. I reach out to pick up Kaila and soothe her.

"Holy shit. But isn't that a good thing? Why are you crying?"

"It's just shocking. Being able to text Nat," I lie.

"Yeah, I guess so," he's looking back and forth between me and the hallway.

"It's ok, go," I say and he lays a loud, wet kiss on my mouth before jogging off to the bedroom to grab his own phone. He reappears, already on FaceTime with his mom, to introduce Kaila and I. I sit next to him on the couch for the next hour as he fills her in on our life here in Hawaii. I stare at my phone on the floor like it's something dangerous and I try not to think about Darren waiting for me on the other side of the ocean or how it makes me feel.

43

MAY 2024

Anna

I'm expecting an announcement any day now saying that we can come home to Canada. According to the news, the President and Prime Minister are very close to releasing a strategy to bring their citizens home. I want to talk about it with Jack and figure out what it means for us – his old life is hundreds of miles away from my old life. Do we even want to go back to those lives? But Jack makes it difficult. Whenever I bring it up, he just says that we can do whatever I want – stay, go, live in Ontario or Whistler or Hawaii; he doesn't care as long as he's with me. It's sweet for him to say but in reality it's unfair for him to lay such a large decision for us both solely at my feet. What about his family? What about his career? I bring it up again and again but get no closer to an answer. My patience is running thin and it shows tonight when I try again after we've had dinner and I've put Kaila to bed.

We sit on our bed and I make sure that there is space between us so we're not distracted.

"We really need to decide what we're going to do when the border reopens."

"I don't care, truly. I just want to be with you so whatever you want."

"Jack, come on, I don't want to make these decisions on my own."

"Isn't that what you wanted from Darren? To make the decisions?"

"*No*, I wanted to feel like I had more of a say in the decisions," I clarify but his flippancy has pissed me off. "So, you're only letting me make the decisions because you want to be better than Darren?"

"Do I *need* to be better than him? Are you rating me against him because you're thinking of going back to him?"

"What the hell? Where is this *coming* from?"

"That's not a no."

"This is ridiculous. Are you only letting me make the decision to test me? To see if I choose home or anywhere else?"

"No," but his voice has a hint of sheepishness to it.

"That's really fucking unfair."

"I said no."

"I don't believe you. And FYI, going home doesn't mean going back to Darren. It just means going home. But he does need to meet his daughter."

"I guess you've made up your mind then."

"Will you come with me?"

"To meet Kaila's Dad."

"If that's how you want to put it, yes."

"So, what does that make me?"

"What do you mean?"

"If Darren's going to be her Dad now, where does that leave me?"

"Jack, I…" I'm honestly not sure what to say. "I love you and I know Kaila loves you, but we haven't even labelled our relationship."

"Uh huh," he grunts. "Anna, all I want is you and Kaila; to be a family. Don't you think that everything else will figure itself out?"

This isn't one of our romance novels, I want to tell him but I don't say anything. Love is great and wonderful and fulfilling but it doesn't build a life. In the real world it takes work and compromise and a lot of fucking communication to meld two lives together, two people with their own visions of what that life is supposed to look like. I want to believe him that our love is enough and everything else will work itself out; I want to believe that life could be that simple. But it wasn't enough for Darren and I, if it was, I'd have never met Jack in the first place.

"So will you be my girlfriend?" Jack asks me when I don't say anything, a smile on his lips and levity lacing his question.

"What?" I ask with a laugh, caught off guard.

"You're right. It's about time we define this relationship."

"Then yes," I say with a smile, leaning over to kiss him.

"I love you, Anna. If you want a plan, we'll make a plan."

"Uh huh," I say in between kisses, "right now I want more of this." I crawl into his lap and hurriedly pull his shirt off.

"How about this?" he lays me down on the bed and kisses my stomach. I moan in reply.

The next day while Kaila has her nap, Jack and I lie on the

couch facing each other. Our limbs are tangled like a soft pretzel. We both admit that we don't know what it will feel like when we return home, if we'll fit into the mold of our old lives or if we want to. We recognize that we can't plan too far ahead without knowing how it will all feel so we decide to fly home as soon as we can and we'll visit my old life first and then his and figure out the rest together.

We don't have to wait long because within a few days the announcement we've been waiting for comes. We can return home. Flights have to be booked through a government website and I have a terrible time because Kaila doesn't have a passport. After spending hours on the phone with a government office, we get it figured out.

Saying goodbye to Lisa is one of the harder things I've ever had to do. It almost feels like I'm losing my mother all over again. When I tell her that she begins to cry too, hugging me tight and telling me I'm not losing her, not at all. We promise to stay in touch and as soon as we decide where to settle, Lisa will come to visit.

44

JUNE 2024

DARREN

Two days ago the government announced that Canadian citizens can come home. I've been waiting for this for more than a year but now that it's here, it feels surreal.

I haven't heard from Anna since service was restored to the US. I feel like it confirms my worst fears – she's moved on. Or she got my texts, including the one where I told her I slept with someone else and she'll never forgive me. Either way, I've lost her.

My phone rings, pulling me from my thoughts. It's Nat. "Hey."

"Have you called Anna?" She asks without any preamble.

"No."

"Oh my god, Darren – CALL HER ALREADY!"

"I can't."

"Why? No, you know what, don't answer that. There is no good reason why! God, this is like every fucking rom-com movie where the two main characters are *dumbasses* that are too scared to tell each other how they really feel!"

"She didn't even text me. And don't try to tell me again that maybe I'm just not receiving them. You get her messages, there's no reason why I wouldn't get mine. If she sent any… but she hasn't."

"Ok well don't sound too jealous there, bud. It's not like she'll take my calls. But it's not about me, it's about you. You should call her, it's Anna, love of your life and you were the love of hers."

"Exactly. Were."

"Oh fuck off, you still are! What did she do, get a quarantine boyfriend? It's not even possible to date without the internet these days."

"You and Chad didn't meet online."

"No but if you hadn't met Anna online than Chad and I never would have gotten together. Ergo, internet was still a requirement."

"That's quite the stretch."

"Darren! CALL HER!"

"Maybe I'll just text her. If she won't talk to you on the phone, there's no way she'll talk to me."

"Fine, I accept but I'm not hanging up until you send me a screenshot of the text."

"Nat, it's fine. I'll do it. I can hear Tanner crying, maybe he needs you."

"Actually it's Logan. He's acting like a big baby because I banned him from watching Paw Patrol for stealing one of Tanner's toys. But that's besides the point. I don't trust you; this is exactly the part in the rom-com where the lead lies to the best friend and the best friend lets them go and then we have to wait all the way until the end for the romantic reunion and there isn't even time for hot make up sex. Don't you want to have hot make up sex? Besides, this is what I have a husband for. CHAD!" She screams away from the phone. I hear Chad yell back but I can't tell what he says. Soon enough though the cries turn into giggles and Nat puts all her attention back to me. "So, what are you going to say?"

"Hey?"

"Oh boy. You're gonna need my help. Just a sec, I'm getting a text. My mom is supposed to pick up the kids so I want – " Nat stops mid sentence and the silence stretches too long.

"Nat, what is it."

"It's Anna."

"What did she say."

"She's flying home tomorrow."

"What? Seriously?"

"That's what it says."

"Tomorrow?"

"Here, I'll just read it to you. Nat, I know you're hurt that we haven't talked on the phone and I'm sorry. I meant it when I said that I can't explain it over the phone. I want to tell you in person and I will very soon. I've got a flight home tomorrow and I'm dying to see you. I'll be flying into Toronto, landing at 3:15pm. Do you think you would be able to pick me up? It's ok if not, but you're the first person I want to see so I'm hoping you can – and then there's the smiley emoji with all the hearts."

"Well, I think you're the real love of her life."

"Shh, jealousy is unbecoming," Nat chuckles. I can tell she's crying, even my eyes feel a little wet. "We're getting her back and that's all that matters."

I want to believe Nat but that's not all that matters to me. I can't just be Anna's friend or worse, her ex. I need her to be my wife, I need her to be the mother of my children, I need her in every possible way. I pull my phone away from my ear just to doublecheck I didn't miss a notification coming through. Nothing.

"What time should I pick you up tomorrow?" Nat asks and I put the phone back to my ear.

"What?"

"You're coming with me, obviously."

"Why? Anna isn't going to want me there."

"You're being a dumbass again." All of a sudden my phone chirps with a text. "Is that a text? Is it Anna?" Nat asks fervently.

"Slow down, give me a second to check. It's her."

"I knew it! What does it say?"

"Hey Dare, it's been such a long time but I'm finally coming home. I fly in tomorrow and I'll be in town for awhile. Can I see you? I'd like to see you."

"No emoji's?"

"No and she only calls me Dare when she's nervous."

"Well of course she's nervous! It's been over a year. But don't worry, when she said I'd like to see you she meant I want your babies."

"What? That's ridiculous."

"I'm her best friend. I know these things. So, what time should I pick you up tomorrow?"

"She doesn't want me there."

"Bullshit. I'll pick you up at 1:30."

"So, you'll be here at 2?"

"Ha, ha, ha. It's not me that's late, it's the kids."

"Sure," I say knowing that's not true at all.

45

JUNE 2024

DARREN

When Nat and I get to the airport it takes us twenty-five minutes just to find parking. When we finally make it to the *Arrivals* gate, we find a huge crowd. Every time the door opens, a family runs forward exclaiming and crying and the rest of the crowd waits in anticipation for their person. I stare at the arrivals board and watch as Anna's flight changes from *Ontime* to *Arrived.* My stomach twists in knots.

After a never-ending wait, a large group of passengers step through the sliding doors and into arrivals. I catch sight of Anna just as she turns her back on us; she's searching the other side of the crowd, hoping to find Nat's face smiling back at her. I recognize the curve of her shoulders and the fall of her hair. I notice how it has lightened after a year in the sun. Nat sees her too and starts waving her arms above her head trying to get her attention even though Anna's back is still to us. I can see someone handing her something which she cradles against her chest and then she turns in our direction. Nat slides her glasses down her nose and then pushes them back up again, not believing what she's seeing. I can't believe it either. Anna's cradling a baby. Her baby.

As Nat and I stand there, slack-jawed and staring, I can tell that Anna has spotted us. I watch so many emotions roll across her face and then the trance is broken as a man wheeling a suitcase stops next to her and slips his free hand into hers.

Anna

There he is, after all this time. I don't know why I'm so surprised to see him. Of course Nat would bring him, hadn't they become besties when the border closed?

I take in the sight of him and time falls away. He's changed – his black hair has grown out until it curls around his ears and a rough stubble darkens his jaw. I feel the same pull of attraction that I've always felt. I see it reflected back in his eyes until he registers Kaila, asleep against my chest. The desire changes to confusion and shock and then his face falls altogether the moment Jack slips his hand into mine. I almost want to pull my hand away but I don't. Jack gives my hand a squeeze and I give him a tight smile before turning and heading towards my past.

DARREN

Nat turns to me with a worried look on her face, "so maybe I was wrong about the quarantine boyfriend," she bites her lip, guilt reflected in her face.

"That's ok. You can't be right all the time."

"Well, I'm not sure – "

"Don't argue with me, Nat," I chuckle in an effort to loosen the tension. "Don't worry about me, Nat. Just go say hi."

"Are you sure?"

"Of course. I'll be here." I can tell that she is torn, not wanting to abandon me but I tilt my head towards Anna and she rushes off to meet her halfway. Anna starts crying before Nat even gets to her and she folds Nat into a one-armed hug, the other arm holding the baby between them.

I watch Anna as she and Nat talk quickly, trying to catch up on a year in the span of a minute in a crowded airport. Sometimes, those two, it's like they're the only people in the room. Anna looks different and yet entirely the same. Her hair is longer and lighter with a kinky wave that looks natural instead of styled. Her skin is tanned golden and spotted with freckles she never had before. And there's something about the way she carries herself, like she's more at ease with herself. She's as beautiful as I remember.

I feel guilty for being here, for crashing her reunion with Nat; I wasn't invited. But I'm still glad I came because I needed to see her. Nat is looking back and forth between me and Anna and they start heading towards us. Anna stops a foot away from me. "Hi," is all she says.

"Hey."

The suitcase-wielding bastard reaches out a hand, "I'm Jack." I stare at his hand for awhile before shaking it.

"This is Kaila," Nat says, pointing to the baby, when no one else says anything.

"Yes," Anna shakes her head as if to clear it. "This is my daughter." She avoids my eyes, looking down at the baby instead.

"She's cute," I say even though I can't really tell. Her face is buried in Anna's shoulder.

"Thanks," Anna says quietly, giving me a quick smile.

Jack lays a hand on Anna's shoulder and she turns to him, breaking the moment between us. "Should we get going?" He asks. I know then that all hopes of a reunion with Anna are gone – she has a boyfriend and they have a kid; there's nothing left here for me.

"Yeah, let's get out of here. You guys must be tired from the long flight," I say, leading the way out of the airport and towards the parking garage. There's an awkward silence between us all as we contemplate the long drive home in a small car.

When we reach the car, I quickly jump in the front passenger seat and sit there anxiously, my knee bouncing up and down, waiting for everyone else to get in and get this over with. Jack is at the trunk loading the suitcases while Nat and Anna are putting Kaila into the car seat behind me.

"She's never been in a car seat before. We walked everywhere," I hear Anna say and Nat proceeds to explain the buckles. When they slam the car door, it wakes the baby and she starts crying. Anna, Nat and Jack are chatting on the other side of the car and don't seem to notice that Kaila's upset. I turn around in my seat, kneeling on the leather and tickle her little socked feet in hopes that she'll stop crying. She just kicks at my hand and cries harder. I start to sing *I Don't Want to Miss A Thing* because I can't think of anything else and it usually works with Nat's boys. Kaila's cries turn to soft snuffles and she opens her eyes to stare at me. Her lashes are thick with tears and her eyes are brimming with more. All the lyrics to the song escape me and my voice disappears as I stare at her, transfixed. Her eyes – my eyes – the same eyes of my mom and my mom's mom. Suddenly Jack opens the car door and slides in, breaking the trance. He wipes the tears from Kaila's chubby cheeks and the world feels especially cruel. "How did you know her favourite song?"

"Huh?"

"I Don't Want to Miss A Thing," he says as if that explains it.

"Lucky guess?"

Anna slides in beside Jack and reaches across him to pinch Kaila's toes. The baby releases a giggle and I turn back around in my seat but not before Anna catches my eye. She knows I know.

Nat climbs into the driver's seat and offers constant chatter the whole drive home so there's no chance for awkwardness. I face forward the whole time, denying every impulse to turn around and stare at my daughter.

46

JUNE 2024

Anna

We drop Darren off first and I feel a painful twist in my gut as we pull up in front of my old house. This whole drive, staring out the window as the city skyline turned into residential neighbourhoods felt so surreal.

Darren jumps out of the car, thanks Nat for driving and looks at me like he wants to say something but in the end he just nods his goodbye and shuts the car door quietly. He stares at Kaila through the tinted window for a moment before turning on his heel and climbing the front stairs two at a time. Nat backs out of the driveway and heads south, towards our Airbnb.

Hamilton used to be unlovingly called the armpit of Ontario but when real estate boomed and Toronto became unaffordable, everyone transplanted and all of a sudden it was artsy and hip and a foodie's paradise. It hugs the western point of Lake Ontario and the Niagara escarpment (referred to as "the mountain" by anyone who grew up here) cuts through the heart of the city. With over a hundred waterfalls and two hundred years of history, Hamilton has it's own charm.

The house that Darren and I bought is in a tidy, downtown neighbourhood called Durand that is full of Victorian architecture. I love it there but I knew I couldn't handle being too close to him so when I booked this trip, I rented us a condo in a tall, glass building on the mountain. This is the area where I grew up although it looked a lot different back then.

Nat drops us off and I can tell that she doesn't want to leave me but does anyway. I want her to stay and I want to tell her every single thing that happened to me this past year but it's been a long day and all I'm good for right now is sleep.

The next day, I ask Jack if he will watch Kaila while I spend time alone with Nat. I feel a little guilty leaving them behind but I can't *really* catch up with Nat if he's there with me. Nat picks me up around noon and takes me to my favourite taco spot. It's just like I remember it and with the rush of nostalgia comes memories of nights here with friends, with family, with Darren.

We get a table on the patio and sit beneath the beating sun. The hostess leaves us with menus but we already know what we want – our orders are the same all the time. We keep the conversation light until the waitress returns with our watermelon margaritas and then we dig into the real stuff.

"So, you had a baby. Darren's baby. But you're with Jack now? I need all the details, especially the sexy ones."

"You can tell that Kaila is Darren's?"

"Oh, so obvious. The eyes are an exact match."

"Such nice eyes. Ok, well I forgot to bring my birth control pills with me on the trip and I didn't even realize and of course we had lots of we-just-got-engaged-sex."

"Of course. Best sex there is."

"Until you talk about what that engagement means and it all falls apart. But you know that part of the story. Ugh. When I found out…I thought Darren was going to hate me, that he wouldn't believe me that it was an accident."

"But it was? You know I'm not going to judge."

"Completely. I don't know *how* I didn't realize I wasn't taking my pills for so long, like come on, I've been taking them for seventeen years, but it didn't register."

"Meh, I've missed so many pills without realizing. And you did have a lot going on in your life; an engagement, a break-up, and then the apocalypse basically. How you ever survived lockdown without Netflix, I don't know."

"I read a lot of books and watched a lot of old movies on VHS."

"VHS? My god."

"Did Darren say we broke up? I didn't really think of it as a break-up. Just a pause, to figure some stuff out."

"Darren? No, he's never wanted it to be over, not this whole time. I just figured it was because you're with Jack, aren't you?"

"Yeah. Now. I didn't want it to be over with Darren either and Jack, well it was unexpected. I didn't know if I would ever get this life back, you know? I had to let myself move forward."

"I get it. That's totally fair. So how did it happen?"

"He was a guest at the bed and breakfast too, from Vancouver so he was stuck there just the same as me. We were friends first and then it got steamy and then I don't know, I felt guilty about it when I was pregnant with Darren's baby. We went back to being friends but we were in love the whole time. Finally, I found the balls to make another move when it became clear that he wasn't going to."

"Aw, you've always had such big balls," she says and we both laugh.

"He's been so amazing with Kaila too. It's like she's his own."

"That's so cute!"

"It is…but I wonder how he will handle co-parenting."

"So you're definitely staying with Jack?" She asks tentatively.

"What do you mean?"

"You know that Darren is an option right?"

"Is he really though? I mean, I know what his texts said but how much of it was real?"

"What texts?"

"He texted me almost every day and then when the network came back, all those lost texts eventually found me."

"Really?! Wow. I thought for sure old texts would be lost. I didn't even know he was texting you. Now I look like a douche for not texting you."

I laugh, "you're not a douche!"

"If you say so. So what did they say?"

"That he still loved me, that he missed me, that he wants to be with me and have a family with me."

"Awwww."

"Yeah, but he also told me he slept with someone. Do we know this bitch?"

Nat barks with laughter, "calm down tiger. We do *not* know her and I'm sure she's fled the country now that you're back."

"How would she know? Do they still talk?"

"I'm just teasing. She's from the US, stuck here just like you were there. So I'm just assuming she's gone home. He never saw her again, never talked to her. Not that I know of anyway."

"Good."

"Says the woman with a serious boyfriend," she teases, a twinkle in her eye.

"I can still be jealous," I retort with a smile.

"Because you still have feelings for him?"

"We've talked *so* much about me; I want to hear about you!" I deflect, not wanting to consider the feelings I may or may not still have for Darren. Ok, definitely still have and definitely don't want to talk about it. Not even with Nat, I need to sort through some of this confusion first.

"I don't know, it was a lot like the first pandemic except that my best friend was missing and I felt lost without her."

"Aw, I felt the same way."

"I can only imagine. You had no one. At least I had Darren."

"Was he really that big a part of your life?"

"Totally. He was the only one who understood this gaping hole in my life where you should have been. And same goes for him. We kind of kept each other together. I told him a lot of ridiculous shit about high school. Sorry, but I had to keep your memory alive somehow."

"You didn't bring out the yearbooks did you?"

"I'm *sorry!*"

"God, he's never going to think I'm cool again!" After a pause, I ask her, "do you think we would have stayed together if I'd come home and C23 had never happened?"

"I don't know. I can tell you that Darren wanted to marry you but he needed more time for kids."

"I don't even know why he wanted to marry me. What made him so ready? After all that time, what changed?"

"You'd have to ask him."

"And he says he wants kids now. At least in his texts. But I'm not sure I believe it."

"Why not? Darren doesn't say things just to say them."

"Oh I know but I just feel like it's gotta be the loneliness that made him want kids. If we got back together and stepped back into our old life, would he really want to be a father?"

"Well, it's kind of too late anyway because he is one."

"He doesn't have to be…if he doesn't want to."

"He wants to, trust me. I believe that he wants a family, for real. You should see him with my boys. You should have seen him when I delivered Tanner. I thought for sure he was going to faint in the delivery room, I mean he can't even handle a casual conversation about mucus plugs, but he was amazing. He got me through it."

"Where was Chad?"

"Ugh, we had this huge fight and he wasn't around when I went into labour and he wouldn't answer his phone."

"About what?"

"The toilet paper roll."

"Oh Nat, not again," I laugh.

"He'll learn one day, I swear."

"So Darren was with you?"

"Every second. I think that's when things changed for him. I could see it on his face, how much he wanted me to be you, for Tanner to be yours, his."

"Oh."

"It's so different for guys. You know Chad and I started our family because he just goes along with whatever I say but Darren is headstrong, fiercely independent, he needs to realize everything on his own terms. And he has. Darren is going to want to be Kaila's father. I guarantee it."

"When I was pregnant, I was sure that he would hate me. That he would say that I did this on purpose, that I was forcing it on him. I was afraid that he would resent me; that he would resent our baby."

"Just give him a chance, you'll see that's not true at all."

"You're probably right."

"I'm always right," she says with a big grin. We spend the rest of the afternoon drinking and eating and laughing as the sun moves its way across the sky. In the end, Chad has to come and pick us up because Nat can no longer drive and when they drop me off, I stumble across the threshold of the apartment, still laughing.

47

JUNE 2024

Anna

Two days later, I wake early, unable to get back to sleep as my mind races, thinking about the day ahead of me. I'm meant to head into Toronto to visit my old workplace and meet with my ex-boss. Apparently, Ace wants me back so I agreed to meet with Melissa and consider returning as a Product Manager but I'm not really sure I want that anymore.

Sick of tossing and turning, I climb out of bed and find Kaila awake and rolling around in her crib. I pack her into the stroller and head out into the bright morning sunshine. Our Airbnb is across the street from a large park that sits along the edge of the escarpment. From there you can see the whole city laid bare in front of you. Kaila and I stroll through the landscaped gardens as the city starts to awaken. I look out over the city I once called home and wish for a view of the ocean. I take in the thick smog of industry, it sits heavily on the skyscrapers and the tall spires of the city's cathedrals. It blurs the rising sun so it's nothing but a hazy ball on the horizon. I continue walking.

Kaila and I met with Darren yesterday in this very park. I reach the final garden and sit on the same bench we occupied in the shade of a gnarled crab-apple tree. I used to come here as a kid so often, having lived so close. Yesterday I felt the urge to climb the tree and see if my initials were still carved into the branch. I put them there when I was twelve or thirteen. I had also wanted to carve the initials of my crush below them – CD – with a heart encircling both but I didn't, worried that he'd find them and he'd know how I felt.

My whole life was lived in this city until Hawaii. I never even left for college, living at home instead. I regretted it at the time, envious of my friends living in dorms and partying all the time but when I lost my Mom, I was grateful for the extra years I had with her.

It felt right somehow to meet Darren here, to properly introduce him to his daughter. Like life was coming full circle. He didn't ask me how it happened or blame me for getting pregnant like I feared. He just held her in his arms and whispered, "I'm your Dad." His voice was steady and confident and full of pride. He told her she was beautiful and that he loved her, that she was everything he'd been waiting for. Nat was right. I can see the change in him. I know he wants a family. With me, with us. I'm reminded of how it felt wanting a baby and being told no, not yet. I thought he should jump in, take a leap of faith, that'd he'd figure it out as it happened. I told him as much, cried over it as much and warned him I might not wait, but in the end I did and I was right to. Because he's ready and he got here on his own terms and it shows. I see it in the protective way he holds her, in the moment where he touches the tip of his nose to hers and how he asks if he can introduce her to his parents. It hurt me to wait – for him, for her – but now we have this beautiful baby girl and it was worth every second. Even if we don't have each other.

Kaila stirs in the stroller, pulling me from my thoughts and I start to head back to the Airbnb.

When I reach our building, I squeeze the stroller into the tight elevator and make our way up to our unit. I find Jack in the kitchen making a pot of strong coffee and I give him a thankful kiss on the mouth. He pulls Kaila out of the stroller and takes her away for her breakfast while I jump in the shower. Once I'm refreshed, I rummage through my suitcase wondering if I have anything work-ish to wear. The best that I can find is a demure sundress. I'll look like a tourist in a city of sleek executives but I find that I don't really care.

I leave Kaila with Jack and head downtown to catch the GO train. I scroll mindlessly on my phone for the hour it takes my train to reach Union Station and I stay seated as everyone else pushes and jostles to be the first off of the train, rising only when the train has emptied. Everyone is in as big of a rush as I remember but not me, not anymore.

I continue to feel out of place as I walk down the crowded streets and ten minutes later, push through the large glass doors of the office building. At first, I think I've gotten the wrong place because it's changed so much since the last time I was here. The open concept has been closed off to create small offices of glass and the rec area that once housed foosball and ping pong and a bar has been converted to small white tables, six feet apart, with one chair at each. A few people I don't recognize sit at random tables sipping Starbucks. I only know I'm in the right place when Melissa comes barreling down the open staircase screeching, "oh my god, it's really you!"

When she reaches me, I can see she is bursting with energy but she keeps her distance except to lean in and extend her elbow my way. At my blank expression she says, "elbow bump, silly!" and in a daze, I reach out my own elbow until ours touch. "I'd hug you but it's against the company's COVID safety policies," she explains.

"I guess that makes sense," I say. She turns quickly and heads back up the stairs and I guess I'm expected to follow so I do.

"Things have changed so much, Anna. But it's better, trust me. We've moved away from open concept as you can see and being back in the office has really improved productivity. We had a few lazy-Lou's so corporate dropped the hybrid work model but the team collaboration now is just *amazing*. Oh, and we've added a whole new department that focuses on helping small businesses. They can get our services for as low as twenty-k! But we did have to implement a sales quota for our Product Managers. Don't worry, it's easy, honestly. You just expand the scope of work with the client once the BDR has closed the sale and boom, there's your revenue." She finally comes to a stop and takes a breath. "Here we are." She squeals and claps her hands, "I'm so excited to have you back."

"Uh, Melissa – "

"Come find me on the fifth floor when you're done and we'll get you a desk."

I stand in the hall, completely bewildered as Melissa jogs to the elevator, her hand raised in greeting to someone else. Her stilettos click-clack against the tile floor and the sound grates on my already frayed nerves. I turn to the office on my right and read *Human Resources* on the open door.

I didn't know what to expect when Melissa reached out on Facebook. I thought maybe an hour over coffee, reconnecting and learning how Ace survived the pandemic; I certainly didn't expect to be rehired and restarting my job *today.*

A man in his early twenties or so (judging by his terribly patchy facial hair) leans over the edge of his desk so he can see around the door and says, "you must be Anna."

"Uh, no, sorry," I say and quickly power-walk down the hall without looking back. Coming here was a big mistake and now I'm stuck in the city, waiting hours for the next train home.

As I speed-walk past the reception desk on my way out, I turn back and ask if Gabby Pérez still works here. Turns out she does. I ask them to page her to the front desk and a moment later, she rushes down the stairs and gives me a huge hug.

"I thought hugging was against company policy?"

"Fuck company policy," she says and I can't help but laugh. For a brief second I think maybe it wouldn't be all that bad to come back here but then Gabby brings me back to earth. "What are you doing here? Once you escape prison, you don't come back!"

I laugh and pull her back into the hug, "it's so fucking good to see you."

"It's so fucking good to see *you*!"

"Do you feel like playing hooky today? I need to kill some time before I can catch a train home."

Gabby fake coughs, "you know, I think I'm coming down with a new or worsened cough," she coughs again for dramatic effect. "It's against policy for me to be in the office with any symptoms." And with that she is pulling me out of the office and into the street. We walk down Queen St, Gabby leading the way and I watch her sleek, short bob flounce with every step.

"I love this new haircut on you."

"Oh thanks! I didn't intend to get it this short but it turns out the stylists who were willing to operate illegally during the pandemic, give terrible haircuts. Had to wait until the salons opened to get it fixed and, well, there was a lot to fix."

"Well, it looks great now."

"Thanks. Oh, we're here. This is my new favourite store."

We step into a sleek boutique filled with expensive clothes and even more expensive shoes. Gabby immediately pulls me towards the shoe section and I find myself staring in shock at the four-hundred-dollar price tag on a pair of white, platform running shoes. I think this style was once referred to as *Dad BBQ sneakers* but apparently it's trendy now. Gabby tells me how she has been lusting after these shoes for weeks and that she has promised herself that she will buy them if she meets her sales quota this month.

"Sounds like a lot has changed at Ace, eh?"

"Ugh, so much. I miss the early days. But whatever, it's a job. It pays for my shoe habit," she glances sidelong at the ugly sneakers as we leave the store and she might even give them a small wave. "Girl's gotta have her shoes."

I used to love my job as a Product Manager with Ace. Melissa was always a bit much but kind enough and the company was new and innovative and I was full of ambition. I intended to make C level before forty. Now I can't imagine spending even one day stuck in that glass box. I don't know what I'll do for work but I'm certain it won't be this.

48

JULY 2024

DARREN

Nat has organized a big home-coming barbeque for Anna as an easy opportunity for her to see all of her friends. Our friends really, and I haven't seen them in just as long. Nat was the only person I could be around this past year.

Anna has been home for more than a week and I've only seen her and Kaila the once. I got a few hours at the park and I'm desperate for more time with both of them. Anna and I have texted some since we met up and sometimes it's awkward but mostly our familiarity gets the better of us and we have our old banter back and forth. I'm still one hundred percent in love with her.

That's what makes it so hard to be here – I'm not sure I can stand to see her with Jack but I wasn't going to miss an opportunity to be with Kaila. I wonder if our other friends are expecting us to be together but I'm sure Nat has explained the situation to them somehow.

I arrive late on purpose, nervous and hoping no one notices as I walk into the spacious backyard. I head straight to the BBQ where Nat is flipping burgers and I give her a quick side hug.

"Hi! I was wondering when you were going to get here."

"Hi to you too and I'm here now."

"Have you talked to Anna yet?"

"I *just* got here."

"I didn't mean *right now*. I just meant; well you know what I meant."

"Yep," I stall, knowing a lecture is coming.

"Darren."

"Nat."

"You need to talk to her."

"What is there to say? She's with Jack."

"That you love her, that you want to be with her, that you want to be *a family*."

"Like I said, she's with Jack. It wouldn't be fair to throw this at her."

"Oh, as if it's not already obvious?"

"Well, if it's so obvious then she knows and doesn't want it."

Nat sighs, "I know you know that's not how it works. She needs to hear you say it. *Especially* after years of you *not* saying it. She has every right to know how you feel, even if it does put her in an awkward position with Jack. That's her call to make. Don't take it away from her."

I know Nat's right but I don't want to admit it. "I think your burgers are burning."

"Oh fuck," she turns around to flip them and I make my escape.

Anna

Jack and I stand in a semi-circle of couples while kids of varying ages play in the grass before us, Kaila included. She's sitting up in the grass but her head is swaying like a bobblehead and it makes me chuckle. Jack picks her up and cuddles her and Kaila lays her head on his shoulder for a rest. *She's such a daddy's girl*, I think and instantly my cheeks grow hot with shame. It feels unfair to think that with Darren on the other side of the yard.

I'm pulled from my thoughts by Michelle asking me when I'm going to be returning to work. I tell her about my visit to Toronto and that I don't know what I'll do but that I can't return to Ace. She asks me if that makes me worried about money and I remind her that I haven't worked in over a year. Her eyes seem to say, *exactly,* but she doesn't say anything else to me, instead the conversation flows around me. It seems to go around in circles talking about careers and comparing renovations and having more kids. I can't help but think that no one seems grateful for what they have.

Jack is as quiet as I am but I'm not too surprised. Back in Hawaii he was friendly and talkative, outgoing and always full of warmth with an easy smile; here he is stoic and shy. He doesn't fit in here, doesn't have anything in common with my friends and I don't think I do either, not anymore.

The guys of the group are saying they're going to get some more beer and they move away from us. Rick calls over his shoulder and asks, "Jack, are you coming?" so he hands me Kaila and follows them reluctantly. Michelle turns to me, seeing an opportunity to pry.

"Jack seems great."

"Uh, yeah, thanks."

"So, things didn't work out with Darren, huh?"

Does she really think I'm going to get into it with her? We were never even that close in the first place, I only put up with her because I've been friends with her husband since we were kids. "Nope."

"But Kaila is his right?"

Is she serious right now? I ignore the question altogether, "So did I hear you got a new house?" I ask. She seems slightly annoyed that I ignore her but just like I thought, she doesn't pass up the opportunity to talk about herself.

"Yes, you've got to come see it sometime! It's huge so you and Jack can stay overnight and Kaila can even have her own room. I guess you'll have to buy a new place now; I'll send you my mortgage broker, just tell them the Francis' sent you. We got such an amazing deal – Rick actually negotiated a lower interest rate. They generally *never* do that but he's such a sweet-talker."

"Uh, congrats," I say, not knowing how else to respond. I don't give two shits about their mortgage rates or their guest nurseries but I want to keep the attention off of myself so I ask more questions. "Did it need any renovations?" I already heard her talk about the reno's but it seems to be everyone's favourite topic and I'm right again.

"Oh, god, yeah! We had to replace the kitchen and the bathrooms when we bought the place because they were *so* two thousand and ten. You should have seen them! Actually you can, I started a blog about home reno's, go to my Instagram. I've already got thousands of loyal followers and they comment the nicest things on my photos."

Just as Michelle is pressuring me to pull out my phone and

look up her blog this instant, Darren saves me. "Hey Michelle," he says stopping next to me.

"Oh hey," Michelle looks gleeful like she expects to have a front row seat to the drama between exes. "I was just telling Anna about my new blog. You follow me, right?"

"Oh, I would never," Darren says nonchalantly, and I have to cover my laugh with a cough. "Can I borrow Anna for a minute?"

"Ok by me but Jack will be back any minute," Michelle says, trying to stir up the drama she's hoping for.

"He'll find me," I say to Michelle with a tight smile and then we make a quick exit before she can say anything else ridiculous. When we are well out of earshot, I shift Kaila to my other hip and lean close to Darren and whisper dramatically, 'thank you." There's a hum between our bodies when we're this close, like an electric current. I felt it the other day at the park when I leaned close to him to take a selfie of us and Kaila. We haven't actually touched since we've seen each other – just come close – and I'm afraid if we do I'll be electrocuted.

"No problem. I know you never liked Michelle and you looked especially uncomfortable now. Do you want me to carry Kaila?"

"Oh, I'm ok, thank you though. Michelle is annoying on a good day."

"And today's not a good day?"

"I don't know, it just feels so weird being here. I miss Hawaii and how simple life seemed. It was such a different experience than what you guys had. Harder, lonelier…but better somehow. The island was just trying to stay alive, stay fed and stay connected to the people we could. No one was worrying about promotions or mortgage rates or how many reno's they could complete under lockdown. No one was trying to get ahead; we were just trying to appreciate what we still had. Does that make sense?"

"Totally." We've reached the patio at the side of the yard where the food and drinks are and Darren opens the large cooler, pulling out a strawberry vodka soda and a beer from the mountain of ice.

"Which one would you like?"

"The beer please," I tease, knowing how much he hates the fake sweetness of vodka sodas. He twists the top off of the beer and hands it over. I watch as he pulls the tab on the vodka soda and takes a deep pull. His face scrunches up in disgust and I laugh. "Just kidding, give me that," I say and we swap drinks.

"That's way too sweet for me."

"It's delicious."

Suddenly Nat is next to us, her hand on my shoulder, "hey, can I steal Kaila for a minute? I want to get some pictures of her with the boys."

"Oh, sure," I say, handing her over and Nat takes off again, leaving me alone with Darren. She doesn't head towards her boys who are climbing on Chad like he's a jungle gym, instead she sits with Kaila at the picnic table and glances over at us. She gives me a big grin and a wink. "I think we've been setup," I say to Darren and he chuckles.

"You know what she's like when she's watching rom-coms? Well, that's how she's treating our situation. She doesn't want us to miss our moment."

I picture Nat throwing her arms in the air and exclaiming at the TV, yelling that the characters are dumbasses. I can't help but laugh at the mental image. "Or else there's no time for hot make up sex! She's got a serious love-hate relationship with rom-coms."

"Exactly," he chuckles before turning serious, "she's right though, I don't want to miss my moment. So, I wanted to tell you – " but he doesn't finish his sentence and I watch as his eyes draw up and away from my face and over my shoulder. I turn around to find Jack walking unsteadily towards us.

"There you are!" Jack exclaims. His eyes are glassy and his smile comes easily.

"Are you drunk?" I already know the answer and I have to admit that he looks damn cute when he's drunk but I still wish he hadn't interrupted us. I wanted to hear what Darren had to say. I wanted our moment.

"I think so. Rick just made me shotgun a beer."

"Oh god, Nat is going to freak out if someone pukes at her party. Those guys aren't twenty anymore – they can't hold their liquor like they used to."

"You might want to go stop them. Someone mentioned something about an old funnel in the garage," Jack says, slinging an arm around my shoulders.

"I'll go," Darren says, "we'll talk another time," he lays a hand on my shoulder as he walks past me, towards the garage and then he's gone along with our moment.

I find Jack a cold bottle of water from the cooler and lead him to a lounge chair by the pool. I tell him that I'm just going to run inside and use the bathroom and he just nods and closes his eyes, settling into the lounger. *How* many beers did he shotgun?

I jog across the yard to the house and head straight for the bathroom, thankful when I find it empty. I stare at myself in the mirror, breathing deeply. I lay a hand on my shoulder were Darren touched me, peeling the fabric of my shirt back to see if there's a brand there because his touch seared my skin. It's smooth and unmarked despite the burning sensation. I splash cold water on my face in an effort to calm myself before leaving. On my way out, I find Nat in the kitchen.

"Hey, where's Kaila?"

"Oh, Darren took her. I hope that's ok?"

"Uh," I glance out of the kitchen window that has a view of the backyard and I can see Darren sitting at the picnic table, bouncing Kaila on his knee. "Yeah, that's fine. Can I help you with anything?"

"I think I'm pretty much set but you can keep me company?"

"That would be perfect. I don't really want to go back out there," I say, pulling myself up to sit on her countertop.

"It's weird, eh? Being around everyone again?"

"So fucking weird."

"I could tell."

"Was it that obvious?"

"Just to me. I know you too well."

"I just can't relate to what they're talking about, you know? How do I even begin to tell them what it was like for me when they're going on about renovations and the latest Netflix show? They wouldn't be able to grasp how untethered or anxious or lost I felt without the internet, without anyway to communicate with you and Darren. They wouldn't be able to get past missing the new season of Ozarks."

"Some of them might. Maybe not Michelle but I think Sarah would. And Taylor. They were very worried about you this past year."

"Maybe," I say absently, picking at the label on the veggie tray next to me. "Do you think I've changed?" I ask out of the blue.

"Changed how?"

"I don't know. Just different."

"A bit, yeah. But it's a good thing. What about me? Have I changed?"

"Not a bit. But it's a good thing," I say and we share a smile.

"So, Jack and Darren in the same place. Is it weird or what?"

"Talk about a mind fuck."

"Did you and Darren get to talk?"

"You mean when you ambushed us? No, Jack interrupted us."

"Do you love him?"

"Which one?"

"Both."

I look out the window, see Darren with Kaila and Jack asleep on the pool lounger. "Yes and yes."

"Oh, you're fucked," she laughs heartily and I join her.

"Yep."

I stay close to Nat for the rest of the night and when the party comes to a close and Jack and I get back to our Airbnb, I curl myself around his sleeping form. It turns out that he snores when he's drunk and it would be cute if it didn't keep me awake. I find myself wishing that he and I could go back to Kauai, back to before the border opened and I learned that Darren was still waiting for me, back to when my life in Canada was a memory and not a possibility. Because now, how do I choose? How do I decide which life to live and what man to love?

49

JULY 2024

Anna

The next morning, I wake up next to Jack groggy and tired. My mind raced for the better part of the night and I didn't sleep well.

"Good morning," Jack whispers on sour morning breath, laying a hand on the small of my back and pulling me closer to him.

"Hey."

"Sleep ok?"

"Not at all. You?"

"Like a baby. Why couldn't you sleep?"

"I just couldn't," I say as I turn onto my back and stare up at the ceiling. "It's so weird being back. It's like I'm stepping into my old life to see if it still fits."

"Does it?"

"I don't know."

"And what about Darren?" he asks quietly and I can feel tears building at the back of my throat.

"I don't know." Jack doesn't say anything in response and I roll back to face him again.

"Jack, I love you."

"I know. But you still love him too, don't you?"

"It's just so confusing," I say and I can feel his body tense against mine. He rolls over and sits on the edge of the bed, facing away from me.

"We could go back to Hawaii, forget about all of this." His voice holds a note of pleading, of desperation.

"We can't," I say and the tears that have been building finally come. I scoot across the bed and lay a warm hand on his back, hoping he'll turn and embrace me but without a word he stands and leaves the room.

I flop face first into his pillow to muffle my scream of frustration. Why did any of this have to happen? Why did the world have to throw another curveball at me? And why couldn't my Mom still be alive to help me? I want to wallow in my pain and tears and self-pity but I hear Kaila crying on the monitor and know that I have to get up and be the mother. Before I go, I send Darren a quick text, *can we talk?*

50

JULY 2024

Anna

The next night I stand in front of my old front door and I keep reaching for the handle and then pulling my hand back. Everything looks the same as it was, the street, the house, even me but nothing is the same. I eventually find the courage to knock and Darren opens the door immediately. How long has he been standing there on the other side waiting for me?

"Hey."

"Hey back," I say, crossing the threshold when Darren steps aside. I bend down to unbuckle my sandals, keeping my back to the wall, conscious of how short my sundress is.

I've left Kaila with Nat this evening knowing that I need to talk to Darren without distraction if I'm ever going to figure anything out. Jack knows I'm here and that I plan to spend the night at Nat's afterwards. We'll dissect everything Darren says over a bottle of wine or two…or three, depending on how this goes.

"I like your dress."

"Thanks," I say timidly, conscious of the tension thick between us.

I follow Darren through the living room and into the kitchen, glancing around me to see if anything has changed. From what I can see, everything looks pretty much the same except that the Xbox has come up from the basement and is hooked up to the living room TV. Our gallery wall has all the same photos – shots of us on various vacations and landscape shots that he's taken. There's one new one though, the selfie of Kaila, Darren and I at the park in a slick black frame. I turn my attention back to Darren as we enter the kitchen.

"How's your family?" I ask as Darren moves to the fridge and pulls out a beer and a bottle of wine.

"They're good. They've missed you." I move around him to grab a wine glass from the cupboard on my left and our fingers touch, sparks flying between them, when I hand him the glass.

"I've missed them too. Alicia's boys must be so big now."

"Practically giants. Nathan is already taller than me."

"Stop it, he is not!"

"Well, he will be. Kid can't stop growing."

"Thanks," I say as he hands me a full wine glass. I take a sip. "Yellow Glen Pink? This is my favourite!"

"I know."

"God, I haven't had good wine since before I was pregnant!"

"No?"

"Hell no. Imports to Hawaii were very sporadic after the border closed and wine was low priority."

"So, tell me about your pregnancy. Was it easy? Or were you hangry all the time?"

"Darren," I gasp in mock anger, "you take that back. I have never, once, in my life, been hangry."

"Uh huh, ok, sure. So, you were definitely hangry then."

"Maybe a little," I say with a laugh. "I had some serious cravings for papaya. Not exactly the easiest late-night snack to obtain when you've run out. Jack had to build up a stockpile."

"Mmm," Darren mumbles, the levity leaching out of our conversation at the mention of Jack.

DARREN

It's tense at first but then Anna and I slip effortlessly into an easy conversation and it feels amazing to hear her laugh. Her dimple deepens even further when she does and I can't take my eyes off of it.

Just as we're getting along, I say the wrong thing and it leads to Jack. The mention of him, the image of him taking care of my pregnant fiancé, cuts like a knife. I take a pull of my beer to cover the hurt and I figure it's time to get into it. I steel myself against the possibility of losing her again. "So," I say. "Should we talk about why you're really here?"

"Uh, yeah," she looks surprised.

"What?"

"Nothing, it's just that you never bring up the hard stuff."

"Oh."

"But, it's good, thank you."

"Ok."

"Ok," she says and we both laugh at our awkwardness.

Anna

"I'm not really sure where to start," I say.

"Start at the beginning."

"Ok…well, when I told you that I was coming home, I hadn't actually figured anything out. Just that I wanted to figure it out together."

"Ok."

"I still wanted you and I still wanted a baby."

"And you didn't know you were pregnant then?"

"No, I found out just before I was supposed to come home. And then the border closed and I was so scared. Of everything, of not coming home, of losing you, of having a baby. I wanted to tell you but I was afraid that you'd hate me or blame me or both, actually. I swear it was an accident, Darren. I never wanted to force you into this."

"I know," he says softly and reaches out his hand, I lay my own in it and he intertwines our fingers. "I'd never think that you would trick me into it. If you were going to do that, you would have done it a long time ago," he jokes and our laughs ease some of the friction.

"Thanks. It means a lot to hear that. Even if it's too late for us, it's still nice to know that you wouldn't have thought that."

"Why is it too late for us? Because of Jack?"

"Everything has changed. I've changed. I'm sure you have too. I don't want to risk what I have with Jack. I love him and he's a good man who loves me, who loves our daughter and I've never doubted that."

"You didn't have to doubt my love either."

I sigh in frustration, "but I did; you made sure of it."

"What the hell does that mean?" He unlaces his fingers from

mine and grips the countertop.

"Like you don't know?! Why did it take you so long to propose to me? What the hell were you waiting for? And why couldn't you move up your timeline to give me a baby? How was I supposed to believe that you were committed to me, that you loved me as much as you said you did, if you didn't consider what I wanted for our future?"

"I always considered it. You don't think it didn't weigh on me? But I couldn't *force* myself to be ready."

"But *why* weren't you ready? I never really understood it; I still don't!"

"Because you wanted a ring more than you wanted me!"

"What?!"

"Fuck! You can be so blind, Anna. I swear." Darren turns his back to me, leans on the island and runs his hands through his hair. "You were waiting for our life to start but we were already in the middle of it," he says, turning back around to face me. "What does a ring or a wedding have to do with commitment anyway? Real commitment looks like waking up next to you every day, making you laugh when your sad or asking about your day, cooking you dinner, offering advice when you complain about work or friends or life. I did all of that – happily – I was there for you; I was *committed* to you. Why did you need a ring so fucking bad? Why did you need to schedule a date to get pregnant? Why couldn't we just live our lives?"

His words hit me like a brick wall and I realize that he might just be right. But the hardest part about realizing your ex is right, is accepting it. That's why I continue flogging a dead horse. "But if we were already living a married life, why couldn't we just have the wedding?"

"We were going to! You needed a ring to see what was right in front of you and so I gave it to you. It didn't mean as much to me but I don't regret giving it to you. It's just that I don't need a ring or a minister or a fucking piece of paper. I just need you, next to me every night and every morning, through the good and the bad."

"But – "

"But what, Anna? But what?! Fuck, why did you even *want* to marry me? If you felt so unloved, why did you want me?"

"I never said I felt *unloved*. It was the complete fucking opposite! I felt *so* loved; more loved than I really believed possible. At least most of the time. The only time I didn't was when you said you weren't ready for marriage. Every time you said that, I second-guessed it."

"I have never not loved you. Not a day since I first told you."

"Well…it felt like I was going to lose you. Like I got everything I'd ever hoped for in a man but I wasn't allowed to keep him."

"You were never going to lose me."

"*Don't* say that, Darren! I could *have*. I *did!* More than a wedding, you weren't ready for a baby. I didn't know if you'd ever be, and I had to make a decision – wait for you and let my time run out or lose you and find another way to build a family. You made me so happy – stupid, crazy, insanely happy. How could I not want to spend the rest of my life with you? But I was going to lose you and it was your fault. Every time you shied away from the future I wanted, I was losing you. Piece by little piece. Whenever you said you weren't ready, it was with such finality. Not up for discussion. And I felt left out of any decisions. That, more than anything, made me feel like you didn't see a future together."

Darren deflates, the anger seeping out of him and he asks, "can I show you something?"

"Yeah? Ok," I say, caught off guard by the quick change in temperature. Darren picks up my hand again and leads me upstairs.

"It's not totally finished yet," he says and then trails off as he opens the door to our spare bedroom. I walk under his outstretched arm and into the room.

"If you still have any doubts that I don't want this then let them go because I want it more than anything. And I want it to be the everything you've dreamed of."

I take in the grey-washed wooden crib on the other side of the room, the black and pink peony wallpaper behind it; I trace the sanded edges of Kaila's name in wood, hanging on the wall and my toes dig into the plush rug beneath my feet. There's a nursing chair in the corner that is begging to be sat in, but I turn away from it and towards Darren.

"How did you – "

"I started it before you even came home. I spent Valentine's Day building the crib and painting the walls. I just wanted to surprise you when you came home, to make you believe that I was ready for this. I didn't expect to have an occupant so soon but when I met Kaila, I knew I had to finish it right away. I hope you don't mind that I creeped your old Pinterest page for ideas. I wanted it to look just the way it would if you'd decorated it."

"I don't mind," I whisper.

DARREN

Tears are forming in Anna's eyes and I can't tell if they're good tears or bad tears but I'm going to let my optimism take over this time. I cross the space between us and pull her to my chest. Her head fits perfectly into the crook of my shoulder; we're like two puzzle pieces coming back together. I can feel her shuddering against me as she's racked with sobs and I let my own tears fall, sliding down my cheeks and into her hair.

I pull away to look at her and she stares up into my eyes. I notice that her tears have pooled in the hollow where her neck meets her collarbone and I all I want to do right now is kiss her there, to dart out my tongue and lap up her tears.

She lays both of her hands on either side of my face and uses her thumbs to wipe the wetness from beneath my own eyes and then she pulls my lips to hers and kisses me so desperately, so hungrily, like it's the last chance she will ever have. I pull her tighter to me, my tongue dancing with hers and it feels like the tide coming in, filling up the empty pools of my soul; it feels like coming back to life.

51

JULY 2024

Anna

"You're home early," Jack greets me at the door with a kiss, as I make my way into the Airbnb laden with Kaila and our overnight bags. I'm calm and my cheeks are dry even though I still feel like crying.

"Mhm, the baby had us up early," I mumble, acting as if I spent the night at Nat's when I didn't. I was sobbing when I knocked on her door at 5:30am and she pulled me into the house, fed me coffee and didn't even ask about the sex.

When I was seated at her dining table with a steaming mug in front of me, she asked me, "are you ok?"

"Not at all."

"That bad?"

I lay my face down on the table. "That good."

"Oh, ok."

"But I love Jack," I whine, looking up at her.

"I know you do…Hey, do you think maybe they would be into polygamy?

"I mean, I never asked," I laugh through my tears at her ridiculous question.

"Would that make them brother husbands?"

When the laughter dies down, I ask Nat the same question I've asked her hundreds of times before. "What am I going to do?"

"You know I love to give advice, mostly unsolicited, but I have no idea what to tell you."

"Do you think I was obsessed with getting married?"

"I wouldn't say *obsessed*…but you were really focused on it. I think you kind of felt like a ring around your finger meant he loved you and the lack of one meant he didn't."

Back when I met Darren I thought I knew what I wanted; what I needed; what life would give me and what it would take from me. But I didn't know anything; maybe I still don't.

"And I know a lot of your issues with timing came down to wanting a baby," Nat continues, "and that is totally valid, we can't stop our biological clocks, but it might have blinded you to what Darren *was* offering. Anyway, who I am to say. It's not like I never told you to dump him or give him an ultimatum. But I regret that now. All I can say is that life is messy and relationships – married or not – take a lot of work and people will falter and make mistakes along the way but you have to remember there's romance in all of that too. I wish I had a crystal ball to tell you how your life is going to turn out but I don't. You're never going to know; you're just going to have to take a leap of faith."

"Is love always this risky?"

"The good kind."

I dump the bags at the front door as Jack takes Kaila from my arms and carries her into the kitchen. "Mind watching her while I have a shower?"

"Yeah, of course."

"Thanks," I say and nothing else. He's going to want to know how my talk with Darren went but I can't get into it until I've washed away the smell, the taste, the touch of him.

Last night when I kissed him it was like I had no choice in the matter, he was an undertow sucking me in like the water does to the sand. He kissed me back as if he's been longing for it since the moment he left Hawaii.

He pushed his tongue into my mouth and devoured me. I knew I'd have to come up for air at some point but I would have been happy to drown in that kiss, the salty taste of his tears on my tongue. When his lips slipped down my neck to my collarbone, I had to pull him back up because I didn't want to breathe in normal air, I only wanted to breathe in his. When he slipped the straps of my dress off of my shoulders and slipped his thumbs in the top of my bra to stroke my nipples I gasped. I remember how that made him smirk, feeling the rise of his lips against mine. I didn't want to wait any longer to feel like Darren was a part of me, couldn't handle the slow burn of foreplay or romance. I hurried to unbuckle his pants, stepping on the ends of them so he could tug them off without removing his hands from my body.

Tripping over our own clothes, we stumbled into our bedroom. The sheets were rumpled and clothes were piled on the chair and it was like time had never touched us. I remember how I walked back towards the bed and fell into it as he leaned over me.

"I missed you," I said.

"I missed you more," he whispered against my skin, his lips on my shoulder.

He kissed his way down my torso and I tried to hide my stretchmarks from him but he gently pulled my hands away and told me I was beautiful.

Touching him was like muscle memory. I closed my eyes and felt every ridge of him; dragged my tongue along every valley. When he growled and cursed with pleasure, I smiled and begged him to be inside me. When he claimed me, it was slow and cautious; until it wasn't.

"Hey, mind if I brush my teeth?" Jack asks, walking into the bathroom and startling me. "Kaila fell asleep in her high-chair so I put her back to bed." He says, grabbing his toothbrush and squirting a line of blue and white paste on the bristles.

"Yeah, I don't think she slept well." I say as I rinse the shampoo from my hair, thankful for the shower curtain between us so Jack can't see how flushed I am.

"So how did it go last night? With Darren? Did you tell him you're not happy here?" And I recognize that this is it, that Jack's not going to wait. He wants me to make a decision about him or Darren, about here or Hawaii while I'm naked and in the shower and he has toothpaste at the corners of his mouth.

"Not exactly," I turn off the tap, my voice suddenly loud without the sound of the water pounding the tiles. I pull the curtain aside and stick my head and hand out as Jack hands me a towel. I wrap it around myself before stepping out of the tub.

"Why not?"

"Well, what does it matter? I can't go back to Hawaii, we wouldn't be able to share custody."

"So, what? All of a sudden he wants kids now?" Jack is

trying to control his voice but there's a sharpness there that wasn't there before.

"It's not *all of a sudden*," I say, sitting down on the edge of the tub.

"What do you mean?"

"He changed his mind about kids before he even knew about Kaila."

"How do you know that?"

"He told me. Well, he texted me. All the time we were apart, he was texting me and when the networks came back, all of those messages delivered."

"And he said he wanted a family?"

"Yeah." I shiver with a chill as the water droplets turn cold on my skin and my hair drips down my back.

"Anna, people don't change. I'm sorry, but they don't. He's going to bail the second it gets hard." That's when I look up at Jack, see the anger screwing up his face. I knew this was going to be hard but I didn't quite expect this.

"They do, Jack. I've changed."

"K, let me rephrase that, *men* don't change."

"I know that you're upset but I didn't even say – "

"What about all the hurt he put you through before that, waiting for marriage, waiting for kids, you're just going to forgive him for that? For leaving you at the airport? For giving you a ring and then *still* saying no?"

I'm pissed by the time he finishes; I don't need Jack mansplaining my own relationship to me. "You know what I've realized? That the world isn't quite as black and white as I thought it was. That I don't have to believe all the shit that girls are told their whole lives – *if a man doesn't put a ring on it, he's not really committed.* And you know what else? A baby doesn't make a family. We were one a long time before Kaila."

"So, what's stopping you from being one now?" Jack spits out.

I think back to a few hours ago, when I woke up next to Darren and something felt off. I slipped out from under the sheets, naked and needing to pee. I tiptoed quietly to the bathroom and looking around me, I saw my perfume and face wash tucked into the far-right corner of the vanity, exactly where I left them. I opened the cupboard door to find my old box of tampons still there and I felt claustrophobic, like the past was closing in on me, trying to mold me back into my old self. But I'm not that woman anymore.

I force myself to look at Jack. A life with him would be so easy but it's not what I want. "It's not you," I say. I know the words are harsh and that Jack deserves so much better than this after everything he's given me. But I'm hurting and I need this to be over. I was never good at break-ups anyway.

52

JULY 2024

Anna

I've realized that I'm still completely, utterly and absurdly in love with Darren and that he feels the same for me. I've already done the hard part and broken it off with Jack. So why am I still so scared to be with Darren?

It's been a tumultuous few hours since sneaking out of his house. Jack has already left for the airport. He'd rather sleep on small bank of plastic chairs waiting for the next flight to Vancouver than be here with me. I guess that's fair. We didn't say much to each other after our showdown in the bathroom and I stayed quiet during his tearful goodbye with Kaila.

I felt sick with regret the entire time, hurting for all of us as I watched him pack up his love and his belongings but I couldn't bring myself to take back what I'd said. Jack reawakened my heart after it's greatest loss and I loved him deeply but seeing Darren again, I realized that it barely touched the depths of me.

And I guess that has scared the shit out of me.

I could run to Darren right now but as much as I want a life with him, I know it can't be here. And how do I ask him to give up everything he has just to be with me? I've got no fucking clue and it's even harder with my old life breathing down my neck. If only I could be back on a beach in Hawaii, maybe I could breathe and figure this out.

I put Kaila down for a nap and sit on the couch in the living room, spinning my phone between my fingers. Darren's been calling but I haven't been answering – finally he gives up and tries texting.

D: why did you leave? Are you coming back?

It takes me awhile to write back.

A: I don't know, Dare. I still love you but so much has changed and I don't know what that means for us. Last night felt more like a beginning than an ending but in the morning, it was just too much. Everything was the same except for me and I just don't fit into that house, that life anymore. It belongs to a different woman, a different life, a different fork in the road. The path my life didn't take.

His response comes quickly, no hesitation.

D: so we'll take the other road. I'll drive.

DARREN

I start to get nervous when Anna doesn't respond to my text. I stare at the screen obsessively, praying to a God I don't believe in to see that bubble of three dots appear but nothing comes.

Anna? I type, my finger hovering over the send button. I don't want to pressure her and I don't want to appear desperate but the truth is, I am. I can't lose her, not again. A minute after I hit the send button, I hear a knock on my door.

I swing it inward to find Anna standing there. Her hair is a mess, her eyes are red and puffy from crying and she's out of breath. Nat's car is parked haphazardly in front of the house and she's alone so I assume Kaila was left with Nat.

"If you're not one hundred – no, one thousand, million, trillion percent *all in*, you better tell me now," she demands, her jaw clenched and her eyes serious.

"Ok, Doctor Evil," I say, my mouth pulled up in a lopsided grin.

"I'm serious, Darren."

I pull her tight to my body, "I'm serious too. I'm one thousand, million, trillion percent all in," and with that I scoop her up, tangle one hand in her hair and bring her mouth to mine. She wraps her legs around my waist and I blink against the tears piercing the backs of my eyes but it's fruitless. They fall anyway.

EPILOGUE

Autumn

2024

SEPTEMBER 2024

Anna

Darren and I have sold the house in Hamilton and moved into a large bungalow in the beach town of Grand Bend on the shores of Lake Huron. It may not be Hawaii, but the beach is only steps from our house, the water is turquoise and the breeze is strong, rustling the grasses of the tall sand dunes. The water's edge is lined with pebbles and sea glass that one day Kaila will love to discover. The property is large enough for yurts or tiny homes and I hope to turn it into a bed and breakfast someday soon. Lisa has already said she will visit in the spring and help me set up the business. She didn't seem at all surprised when I told her that I had gotten back together with Darren, actually she expected it; call it mother's intuition, she said.

It was harder than I thought selling our old house, saying goodbye to all of the good memories and especially the new nursery but Darren promised to replicate it exactly in our new house and he's kept that promise, making sure it was ready for our first night here – tonight.

We've gotten into a routine where we put Kaila to bed together, snuggling three to a chair and reading her books, taking on a character each and giving them their own, silly voices. Tonight is no different and when Kaila's eyes close for the night and I watch Darren lay her in the crib with a soft kiss to her crown, I feel down to my bones that I am finally home and so is she.

We leave her to her dreams and Darren follows me through our bedroom to the ensuite where I've drawn us a bath in the large soaker tub. We slip beneath the bubbles into the steaming hot water, Darren behind me with his arms wrapped around me as I settle against his chest. He holds me as I cry for all the time that we had lost and when all the tears are gone, I turn around and ease myself onto his lap and we give each other all the love that we had pent up.

Afterwards I lie in bed in his arms, wide awake as I listen to his breathing become deeper and deeper. I play with his chest hair and marvel at the ease with which we have slipped back into our relationship. I wear my engagement ring but I don't know if we will end up having a wedding or if we will have more kids or anything else the future holds. But I'm ok with that. I don't need to plan for the future anymore, I just want to live in the moment because as I've learned, the future is never guaranteed. All we have is today.

Manufactured by Amazon.ca
Bolton, ON

36027293R00155